THUNDER 

Our response to Da
was just wonderful.
sold the last one the other day. (I was kind of holding on to it, happy I did for my customer. Her husband forgot to tell her we had the book in stock! He would have been in BIG trouble.) Have a wonderful new year!
Cheryl
Cheryl's Old Book Barn

WHAT THE CRITICS ARE SAYING. . .

"Dara Joy . . . sets our hearts ablaze with a romance of incandescent brilliance. An electrifying talent!
-Romantic Times (Rejar)

"There is a rising star in the genre who absolutely does not write books that are similar to any others and that is Dara Joy, an author who [was] literally an overnight success..."
-The Romance Reader

"Hip, Hip, Hooray! Dara Joy has done it again! This author has one of the truly inventive and devious minds in the romantic field. This book is a sterling example."
-The Ridiculous Book Store

"An author who skillfully hides sub-text under inventive

storytelling is, to me, a highly talented author, and I doff my hat to the Joys of the world who manage to do this. Her stories have a staying power that is incredible and every single time I go back to one of them, I find something new that jumps out at me. This is multi-layered."
-All About Romance

"If you love great stories with great characters you're going to love Dara Joy."
- Jen's PLace

WHAT READERS ARE SAYING ABOUT
'THAT FAMILIAR TOUCH'. . .

That Familiar Touch will be read again and again just like the rest of her books. . . I can't get enough of her books.
Kym

I just thought I'd drop y'all a line... Living along the Alabama coast we had a really scary time of it lately with Hurricane Ivan breathing down our neck. As I was (trying) to prepare my room for the storm, of course, I put several items that are irreplaceable into a waterproof shoebox and shoved it into a bottom corner of my closet. Included were bank statements, various diskettes with my fanfiction, and in a zip lock baggie: my copy of That Familiar Touch. I just thought you might want to know that even faced with the possibility of serious house damage, that book is well worth protecting.
Sincerely, Rita

I just had to get my hands on anything that had DARA JOY printed across the cover. Not one of your books has disappointed me... and that is saying something. Thank you from the bottom of my heart for your courage and endless devotion to your fans. Much love and support, Amy

Dara,
I'm sure you must be flooded with emails right about now but I just wanted to let you know that I ABSOLUTELY LOVED this book and I'm eagerly anticipating any more that may be forthcoming from you.
Stay Strong, Mari

Dear Dara,
The book was fantastic and worth the wait. As long as you keep writing I'll keep reading. Your books are all keepers. I tell everyone how great they are but I'm afraid to let them out of my sight. Some people don't return and I would have a fit. . . I will read "That Familiar Touch" again and then read all your previous books for the tenth time. Love, Love, Love, your work.
A big thank you from Catherine

I read THAT Familiar Touch it was beautiful but I need MORE! . . . I love you Dara!
MAGGIE

I thought TFT was a brilliant book and I loved reading more about the characters from the previous MOD books. . . I also thought KpW was a very special story filled with so

much hope for any one who's been through tough times. I would definitely buy any more novels or novellas you write wherever they were available from. . . Keep fighting and please let me know if there is anything I can do to support you in your fight against Dorchester. Looking forward to the next book!!!!!!
Rachel / Raci

Dear Dara,
I enjoyed That Familiar Touch as I did all your books. I appreciate the effort that went into creating it and getting it to your readers. You have the rare ability to create new worlds and draw the reader in. . . It's rare to find authors who can create plausible settings and tell a good story. After I read the first couple of your books, I was hooked. . .
Best regards, Rebecca

IF YOU WOULD LIKE TO WRITE TO US PLEASE SEND EMAIL LETTERS TO QASK89@PRODIGY.NET
OR SNAIL MAIL:

HOUSE OF SAGES
P.O. BOX 850033
BRAINTREE, MA 02185

COME VISIT DARA'S CASTLE AT
WWW.OFFICIALDARAJOY.COM

SEE YOU THERE!

THE AMAZING TALES OF WILDCAT ARROWS

Dara Joy

Other House of Sages books by Dara Joy:

THAT FAMILIAR TOUCH

This is a work of fiction. Names, characters, places, and incidents are products of the author's imagination or are used fictitiously and are not to be construed as real. Any resemblance to actual events, locales, organisations, or persons, living or dead, is entirely coincidental.

ISBN: 0-9753549-1-4

 For information address House of Sages at INFO@OFFICIALDARAJOY.COM
House of Sages trade size paperback November 2005 FIRST PRINTING, FIRST EDITION.

Visit Dara Joy on the World Wide Web at WWW.OFFICIALDARAJOY.COM

Printed in United States of America

This book is dedicated to the noble dachshund: a canine who wields silliness as his weapon of choice.

To all of my fantastic readers,

If anyone had told me that I would set up a publishing company and publish my own work– not once but twice– I would have thought they were writing the fiction. Yet, here we are.

This has been a difficult but rewarding experience. I've learned that books are much like children. Each one is unique with its own temperament– and each one is birthed differently. I am so happy this 'baby' is finally out and in your hands. Despite the travails of the process, it is very satisfying to create new stories for those who truly adore this kind of fiction. Many of you have asked me to continue producing original stories in this manner. I will leave that– as I always do– in the hands of the readers. My pen is ever on standby for your reading pleasure.

All of us at the House of Sages want to thank you for your loving support. May all the hard efforts of writers and readers alike continue to keep our beloved books alive.

Love,
Dara

THE AMAZING TALES OF

WILDCAT ARROWS

This work is based on an entirely fictional universe. Any similarities between places, events, characters, and the laws of physics depicted herein to the universe as we know it would seem highly unlikely.

Table of Contents

Unpaid Advertisement

The Amazing Tales of Wildcat Arrows is sponsored by *Getitall.*

Getitall, guaranteed to achieve for you what you think you deserve.

Not getting that promotion you desire? Tired of more talented stooges passing you by on the Corporate groove to the top? Fret no more! You've discovered *Getitall*!

See what our happy customers are saying about this fabulous product:

Testimonial: *"I was a no account loser stuck in the sub-sub-basements for eons until I tried Getitall! Now I'm an up and coming climber, achieving subbasement with no end in sight!" Ima Flunky, Bose Idahoee II**

Another great testimonial: *"Unfortunately, I was at the end of my tether. Things got so bad I even considered ending it all by quitting my job. Then I got Getitall and I am so glad I did! The very next day I got a longer tether." Gravlax Smukli, Kankachee II**

Why wait a moment longer? You could already be on the winning team! Order *Getitall* now.
Getitall is brought to you by SysCorp. "You've got a friend in SysCorp!"

**testimonials may not be factual*

WILDCAT ARROWS

For some reason, I was stimulated by marketing and fascinated with how commercials would sell a product. So I got my degree in marketing.

- Carrot Top

HOW IT USUALLY STARTS

Planet Volauvent

"Director! Director!"

Somewhat annoyed at the interruption, Big Gun put the portfolio he was studying aside to acknowledge his No. 1 Stoolie. The man's company knowledge was vast but he greeted every concern as a matter for hysteria. "Yes, what is it, Heiner?"

"A catastrophe, Superordinate One! A catastrophe!" He slid up to the platinum dais, coming to an abrupt stop with a screeched brake of his feet. He almost toppled over the stone balcony on the other side.

Big Gun arched a brow. What was it this week? Too many bidding on the floor? A surfeit of commodities on the company ledgers? An imminent attack by a rival consortium? Or too much spice in the evening meal?

With Heiner it could be any one of those things as he perceived each one with the same level of gravitas.

Big Gun waved his arm motioning the distraught man to slow down and take a breath. The Day of Investiture was fast approaching– only a few months were left before the capstone of the Whatnot Consortium was firmly and irrevocably placed in his hands.

He had proven himself for three years, as law demanded.

It was time for him to take permanent control. The directors of all twenty-nine corporations had patted his attaboy head and agreed that he would be the next ascending member to the royal board of Whatnot.

There were speeches to write.

Lots of speeches. As far as Big Gun was concerned, this interruption was not well-timed.

"Relax, Heiner," Big Gun remarked drolly, magnanimous and patient in his finest hours. "I am sure nothing is so dire that you must kill yourself before imparting it to me."

"Oh, but it is, your Superordinate One! The-the-" Heiner's face flushed bright red; his eyeballs began to roll back in the sockets.

The clodpole was about to pass out.

"BREATHE!" Big Gun commanded. "One, two– out. One, two– in." Big Gun impatiently waited for his No. 1 Stoolie to gather himself.

"It is the Heart of the Merchandiser!!" Heiner finally burst out.

Big Gun blanched. This was the last thing he was expecting. His voice dropped in cadence. "What of it?"

"It is missing!" Heiner started wringing his hands.

"*Missing?* What do you mean it is missing?"

No. 1 snapped his fingers. "Gone. Just-like-that."

"But- but that is impossible! It is guarded night and day!

How could this have happened?"

"We don't know. Everything was fine one moment and then the the guards found themselves waking up from a sound sleep! They have no memory of what transpired! Oh, Director, what shall we do? *The Heart of the Merchandiser!*" He wailed, just in case Big Gun was not appreciating the full horror of the situation.

Big Gun sat back in his director's chair and rubbed his jaw. *This is serious indeed.* Without the Heart of the Merchandiser he could not be named "the true and righteous Poobah" of the consortium.

Worse than that, the by-laws decreed that who so ever possessed the Heart of the Merchandiser on the Day of Investiture would be claimed Incomparable Honcho.

Big Gun closed his eyes. He was more concerned about the fate of Volauvent should some unscrupulous person– one who could steal the Heart of the Merchandiser itself– actually ascend to the head of the company. He loved his employees, and they him. Volauvent was scheduled to get many boss-perks because of his promotion. For one, Whatnot had promised every citizen of Volauvent a free housecleaning quarterly. Should the people find out they might not be getting that– well, it would be *terrible.*

There would be an uproar.

He recalled the anti-clutter riots of '09 with a shudder.

And surely such an unscrupulous thief would not be concerned with the company's best interests?

Unlike many Corporations, it was Whatnot's core policy that a Director could not manage his employees wisely without at least giving the *appearance* of caring about them. The Heart of the Merchandiser, the purest, largest, inclusion-free hunk of miadne stone ever found, was the symbol of everything that Whatnot stood for.

"Profit with commiseration!" was not only their motto; it was their entire advertising campaign.

This was a dire situation indeed.

"What shall we do? What shall we do?" Heiner carped over and over.

Big Gun's stroked his jaw, his shrewd business acumen swiftly coming into play. "Did the guards find anything unusual? Anything at all?"

"Just some scratches where the miadne was housed. Our forensics experts examined the area for prints, fluids, fibers. . . there was nothing. Whoever took it was highly skilled."

"How did they get past the lasers, the cameras?"

Heiner shrugged.

Big Gun pushed a button next to his chair. An image of one of the forensic examiners shimmered in front of him.

"Sir?"

"Let me see the images of the scratches."

"We couldn't make anything of them, sir. They appear to be just random markings. Probably from when the stone was pried loose."

"Just let me see it."

"Right away, sir."

An image of an empty pedestal formed in front of his face. Two sets of scratches were dug into the base on either side of the housing. The left side featured two series of scratches truncating from the end of a main line. The right side had two identical lines radiating out at an angle from a single point.

Big Gun snorted. He reached out and grabbed the edge of both images, folding it over and onto itself so the scratch lines joined. "What does that look like to you, Heiner?"

Heiner squinted at the images. "Arrows, sir?"

Big Gun leaned back in his chair, crossing his arms over his ample belly. "Exactly. *Arrows.* And who is the best tracker in the galaxy?"

"Um. . ." Heiner's face screwed up in confusion. "That would be Wildcat Arrows, Sir."

"Exactly."

"But he couldn't have had anything to do with this! He's been incarcerated for the past six months on Cretion."

Heiner's vast knowledge of mundane facts and his ability to toss them up at lightning speed never failed to impress Big Gun. The man was a living, breathing search engine.

"Doesn't sound like him. What's he in for?"

"That is not altogether clear."

"I see." Big Gun stroked his jaw. "Arrows is definitely connected in some way to this theft and I'm going to find out just where he fits in. Those scratches are no coincidence. Someone left a cartouche for us to find. Get me the warden on Cretion; I want to speak to Wildcat."

Heiner punched a code into his pinkypod. A low conversion ensued.

A few seconds later Heiner looked up with a puzzled frown. "Arrows escaped earlier today."

Big Gun arched his brow. He was surprised and, in a begrudging way, impressed. "From a Class One security prison?"

"A first, I believe."

"Mmm. He *is* good. Were any ships able to leave Volauvent before the lock-down?"

"Just one."

"Where did it go?"

"Slide."

Big Gun nodded curtly. "Start there. And see if you can find any other connection to that ship. Overlook no detail. There has to be something on our surveillance cameras."

"Yes, sir!"

After Heiner left, Big Gun stood up and paced the entire length of his cavernous work chamber.

He had been a well-loved Director, having proven himself cunning in all matters of business. This planet enjoyed an excellent trading level because of his shrewd dealings.

But that could all end if he didn't get the Heart of the Merchandiser back!

Well, he still had plenty of secret contacts. . .

He was not going to let this spurious theft get the better of him!

Not without a fight.

Should Arrows have gone completely underground and disappeared. . . Well, he would need an alternate plan.

A worthy plan.

And if that did not work– there would be some serious paybacks in order!

Appropriately, the first name on that 'to-do' list started with an "A".

EPISODE ONE:
FORTUNE FAVORS THE BOLD

Somewhere in the galaxy 2036, e.t. (Earth time)

"Where are we?"

"I have no idea."

Lucky Red stretched in her chair and crossed her booted feet over the command console of her ship.

Well, technically not *her* ship.

That scoundrel Wildcat had disappeared on Cretion over six months ago and left them to deal with it!

The motley crew he had assembled over the years had to make their way across an unforgiving galaxy without benefit of their savvy Captain. No one seemed to have any information as to his present whereabouts.

As she crossed her hands behind her head, the worn denim covering her shapely legs pulled taut. From covered wagons to intragalactic space ships, blue jeans had survived. Lucky had on her standard uniform: a black vee neck tee, wrangler jeans and her favorite 'jangling' Justins.

The silver buckled straps twining around the insteps of the black boots clinked 'real *purty'* when she moseyed into a cargo bay.

Exactly like Wildcat had taught her.

To the rest of the galaxy, there wasn't anything as terrifying as a Texan moseying in space.

At least according to her brother, who had witnessed the horrified fascination first hand.

She did love to see all those amusing alien expressions when they found out that her Justins were still made from *gen-u-ine* animal skin.

She was an Earthgirl and proud of it! Damn straight.

So what if Earth was the butt of every sorry joke in the galaxy? And, she had heard them all.

What's the difference between a garbage troller and Earth?

Nothing.

Why did the Kraogian Ooze Sucker defer to the Earthling trader?

Professional courtesy.

How many Earthlings does it take to change a rocket sprocket?

All of them. First they must argue whose sprocket it is then they kill each other off for the chance to change it.

She was heartily sick of it! So what if the rest of the civilized planets considered Earthlings barbarians? It certainly didn't stop them from being *interested* in Earthlings.

"Maybe Clugot knows where we are?" Lucky sighed, not expecting a positive response.

SpinDrift pursed his soft beak. "Why would Clugot know? He never leaves the engine room!"

Oh well. Floops were kind of a weird group. And of all the weird-ass Floops in the galaxy, SpinDrift took the prize. Even other Floops thought Spin was kind of *odd*– so that said it all.

"You never know. I'll check." Lucky leaned forward and pushed one of the purple buttons on the panel in front of her.

Clugot's square head filled the screen along with his perpetual, blank stare.

"Urrr?" Came the deep, scratchy voice.

"Clugot, do you know where we are?"

"Urr."

"Okay, thanks anyway." She flipped off the link.

SpinDrift waddled over. "Well, what did he say?"

"Um, he said *urr*."

"That's all he ever says!" He started to walk away then stopped. "Wait! Two 'urr' sounds or three?"

"Ah, two, I think."

SpinDrift nodded and gave her a superior look. "I told you he wouldn't have a clue."[1]

Lucky's jaw dropped. "You didn't know that and you don't know that."

"Not so! Not so! I do know it and I did know it!"

Several feathers launched themselves off the crest of Spin's head like insouciant kamikazes.

A usual occurrence when he was in high dudgeon.

Alas, SpinDrift was in high dudgeon just about most of

[1] With Kelvinators, the longer the "urr", the more definitive the response. The worst possible response was, 'ur'; which in essence could be anything. *So? Maybe? Big deal?* No way of knowing exactly; the general meaning must be inferred. Unlike 'urr', which was generally perceived as a 'no'.

the time and, thus, appeared to be in continual molt.

But only on the top of his head.

Shoot! Nothing had been the same since her brother, Wildcat, had pulled a Jimmy Hoffa on them. They had been wandering aimlessly through space for almost six months! She had persistently tried to get information out of the Cretion authorities. After months of getting nowhere, she had been curtly informed today that he was no longer on the planet!

Well, then where was he?

The Cretion governor refused to let her dock the ship or even enter their space, citing some kind of new quarantine restriction involving a nanite infection.

If Wildcat had left, he had not tried to contact the ship.

Which was very unlike him.

They had no way of knowing where he was, whether he was alive or not, or when he would return.

She sighed. What had he been doing on Cretion in the first place?

With his clandestine dealings, it could have been anything.

He wasn't called 'Wildcat' for nothing.

Her rascally, devilishly handsome 'brother' might have finally got himself into trouble he couldn't sweet-talk his way out of.

She wiped a tear from her eye.

Heck, he was a good enough brother. Different from most and not what you'd expect out of an older sibling. Still, he always took care of her and made sure she had a belly full of food. Even when he didn't.

So, SpinDrift's latest glib reply was all that it took. Lucky jumped the couch.

"Argh!! I'm going crazy out here! If we don't do something–"

"I know what *your* problem is!" He wagged his claw at her.

Oh, geesh. Here it comes. Pearls of funktified wiz-dumb. Lucky crossed her arms over her chest waiting for the birdbrained salvo.

"You must have some Earthling sexual activity immediately."

"You are a cluckhead."

"Hmph. I've read that Earth people like you *need* sex on a constant basis. Why, I–"

"I do not need sex! Well, I mean I would like it, but I am not– *Where do you get this stuff?*" There are those who love to love and those who are in love with love. Lucky supposed SpinDrift was in the later category. To a Floop, there was nothing better than love filling the air and romance blossoming. It made them flutter up a storm.

"Ahhh! You see! If you want accurate information, you read *Kick It to the Cosmos!* I don't know why you refuse to subscribe. It is very informative." He placed his twiggy arms on his feathery hips. "The last issue discussed twelve ways to make your fab Floop feel like he had a zero gee org-"

"Give me a break! That stuff is all crap. I don't know why you even read it."

"Pft! They are the true geniuses of the galaxies, I tell you. And I was basing my observations on your brother, for your information."

"Oh, nuts. Don't go by *him*."

"But now that *you* brought it up– a female Earthling of your age who has not engaged in sexual activity is a most bizarre specimen-"

"You're calling me bizarre?!" She burst out laughing.

She had been eight years old and swooping low back and forth over the surface of Pittipat– without her brother's knowledge, of course. That's when she spotted the Floop running for his life.

Feathers flying everywhere, shrieking.

She had hovered over SpinDrift, sent out a perimeter pulse barrier and brought him onboard. He had been a member of their small crew every since.

Wildcat had been furious with her for taking the ship out of drydock while he got supplies. He was even more furious that she had taken on a Floop.

Once taken into one's life. . . they never leave!

Floops insinuate themselves into every aspect of their host's life and generally make themselves into huge nuisances.

How was she to know? She was just a kid.

At first, her brother tried everything he could to get rid of the cleaving noodge. Like a garbage-skow barnacle, SpinDrift held steadfastly on.

Finally Wildcat gave up and acclimated himself to the situation. Her brother usually had the wisdom to know when he could not make a difference.

Besides sticking like glue, it seemed that Floops also loved to bicker. Pick. Pick. Scratch. Scratch.

Which was undoubtedly why he was being run out of town by those villagers in the first place.

That was ten years ago and the 'itch' was still here. She suspected he would hang with her for the rest of her life.

Wildcat was not happy at the turn of events. Not happy at all. Whenever he referred to SpinDrift it was usually *"That birdbrained itch!"* or *"Vacuum-noodled feather heap!"* or. . . Well, he had a hundred of them.

"What is *wrong* with a little love?"

Ugh! He was like a dog with a bone! "Do not confuse love with sex, SpinDrift."

"La grande ambition des femmes est d'inspirer le sex!"

Lucky pinched the bridge of her nose. Oh no. He was quoting *him* again. Molière didn't have a chance.

SpinDrift was fascinated with Earth culture of the last four hundred years. Lately, he had taken to watching old BBC mysteries.

He was utterly convinced he could become a great detective. All he had to do was follow the lead of such daring sleuths as Miss Marple and Hercule Poirot.

Especially Hercule.

In a disturbing twist, SpinDrift had taken up quoting the good Monsieur. Always at the most inappropriate times.

Unfortunately, SpinDrift's Poirot quotes never were quite. . . right. At least he had finally moved on from his last fixation: Bruno, the Austrian fashionista.

Thank goodness Wildcat wasn't here for this latest fad of his. Her brother might have wrung Spin's scrawny neck for real.

"Just how do you know I haven't had sex anyway?"

Apparently sex was the key to all romance. Floop style.

SpinDrift crossed his spindly arms and gave her another knowing look. He pointed his claw to the ceiling, proclaiming in a terrible Belgium accent, "Exactement! It is absurd - improbable - it cannot be. So I myself have said. And yet, my friend, there it is! One cannot escape from the facts!"

Help. He was nutzoid over that weird little detective!

Still, he was right.

Lucky's lower lip jutted out.

She threw her arms wide with frustration. "You *know* that Wildcat and Cloud scare off every potential candidate! What am I supposed to do? None of them are good enough to be trusted– according to them."

SpinDrift shook his head sadly. "Tsk-tsk. Would that your brother was as particular for himself! I will work on him later. But *Sensei* Arrows is correct in his approach."

Despite the fact that Wildcat barely put up with SpinDrift, the Floop firmly believed that the infamous tracker had taken him on as some sort of mystical student.

Of what, was anyone's guess.

"You haven't chosen your acquaintances carefully in the past, Lucky."

"What do you mean?"

"You do remember that happy lad from Crionoutlud?"

Lucky's shoulders squinched. "I don't want to hear it." As usual, SpinDrift ignored what she said and went relentlessly on.

"Wasn't he the coy one with his *twenty-seven* wives?"

"Look, not everyone is perf–"

"And then there was that lusty fellow from Tuber Tang."

"*Stop.*"

"Something about his poisonous stinger, wasn't it?"

As if she could forget *that* fiasco.

Lucky exhaled noisily. "I never should have come to your rescue all those years ago."

"Maybe it wasn't such bad a thing Sensei Arrows stepped in to stop you when he did?"

Lucky agreed with SpinDrift on that one.

The autonav system interrupted their latest, tenth spat of the day.

"ATTENTION! MINMEI MUST HAVE ATTENTION! INCOMING MESSAGE! TEE-HEE-HEE."

Lucky actually sneered at the computer. The stupid thing sounded like a character out of a 1990's anime. Wildcat had bought it on the cheap from Mama Bros Not Quite Used Emporium.

No telling where that thing had been.

"TEE-HEE-HEE. HERE IS THE COMMUNICATION. I'LL SING FOR YOU LATER AT MY NIGHTLY CONCERT, MISS LUCKY."

Minmei had one song. That she repeated. Over. And over. And over.

Usually when Lucky was trying to go to sleep.

"Shoot! I thought Clugot finally erased that from her memory."

"*Ooooo,* a message!" SpinDrift's switched from pestering to ecstatic nosiness. "Go see what it is! Hurry!"

"All right." She flipped the channel open.

"Greetings! I am seeking Arrows, the well-informed and discerning tracker."

"Arrows the well-informed and discerning tracker?" Lucky rolled her eyes at SpinDrift. "I think someone is looking for dear bro."

SpinDrift scratched under his beak. "Someone's always looking for Sensei Arrows."

Lucky agreed. "And that ain't always good."

"Is anyone there?"

Lucky leaned forward. "I'm sorry, you have the wr-*mmyph!"*

SpinDrift covered her mouth. "Ask why they want him first."

Probably a good idea. She removed his claw by clasping the wrist, her pinky pointing up in mock disgust. "What do you want with Arrows?"

"Allow me to introduce myself. My name is Heiner. I am calling for the Big Gun of Volauvent."

SpinDrift squealed behind her. "The Big Gun?! He's huge! Find out what he wants, Lucky, quick!"

Lucky kicked his spindly leg to shut him up. "Go on, Mr. Heiner."

"Just Heiner, please. It is with deep regret that I inform you that the wondrous Heart of the Merchandiser has been stolen."

Now *that* was huge.

So Spin was right. But why were they contacting the Sugarbabe?

"We have heard of your impressive reputation as a *solver*, Arrows. We wish to hire you to track it down."

"*Me*? No, no, you don't understand; I'm not– *mmmxph*!"

SpinDrift covered her mouth with his claw again.

"Wait! Let's hear the rest!"

". . . I am instructed to offer you a great reward if you will agree to accept this case."

"A case!!!" SpinDrift almost swooned. "Just like Poirot!" He assumed the Belgium accent. *"It is my weakness, it has always been my weakness, to desire to show off!"*

Lucky stopped thrashing and removed SpinDrift's claw from her mouth once more. "Will you quit that?" she hissed. "Geesh, let me talk to him." She turned back to the caller. "Um, Heiner, exactly what kind of reward are we talking about?"

"We have agreed that a suitable prize for finding and returning the Heart of the Merchandiser must be one that almost equals our beloved jewel. There is another jewel we hold dear on Volauvent. To show our serious intent on reclaiming our Heart of the Merchandiser– and to remove temptation from the reclaimer to sell elsewhere– we will offer an exchange of the Heart of the Merchandiser for the *Heart of the People."*

SpinDrift's wiggly eyes twitched to the back of his head. The prospect of all that potential wealth was causing the blood to vacate his brain.

The floop-a-zoid started to pass out.

His wings managed to flutter one last time in a cackle of excitement just before he went out cold. He hit the metal floor like a gravity bomb.

Lucky waved at him to keep the noise down so she could hear the rest of what Heiner was saying.

"This Heart of the People. . . it's worth a lot?"

"Some say it is as priceless as the Heart of the Merchandiser."

"Wow."

"So, do we have a deal, Arrows? Will you bring us back our special jewel?"

Lucky bit her lip. They obviously wanted her brother.

Where was he? Something had to be wrong; he *never* would have abandoned them. He hadn't done it in the past and he wouldn't do it now.

It could not have been easy for Wildcat to care for her–they had been run off Earth when she was still a squirt. In fact, he hadn't even known he was going to take responsibility of her until she was handed over to him one windy morning. As her mother lay dying, she had entrusted her baby's well-being to the smooth-talking, beautiful rebel she had come to trust.

Wildcat embraced this fate as he did most things that came his way.

He simply smiled that winning smile of his and tied her onto his back, papoose-style. He had told her they were off to make their fortune in the stars.

That was over eighteen years ago.

He still told her the story every now and then. Lucky wiped another tear from her eye.

The Cat had accepted total responsibility of her because . . . well, he was just like that.

It wasn't hard to see why her mother had entrusted her to him. Wildcat had a way of getting into people's hearts and stayin' there.

Not that he tried to do that, mind you. Surely, if he was told of it, he would be completely mystified.

He did not even know her name– and neither did she, so he called her Red because of the little tufts of crimson fuzz on top of her head. He named her *Lucky* because he told her that the day she was handed to him was the luckiest day of his life. Not only had he discovered new kin, he told her, but he realized that in order to make a life for both of them he would need to start over.

Babe in arms, he took to the skies.

Back then, Earth was for the rich and powerful. The poor had to make do as best they could. Once contact was made, all kinds of opportunities opened up for those who had the guts to go for it.

And go for it, Wildcat did.

On Earth, he was recognised as an expert *finder.* People, oil wells, you name it. But he didn't like working for the corporations.

Still didn't.

In five short years, he had used his talents to become the owner and Captain of his own interstellar spaceship. The *Sugarbabe.*

Rumor had it he won it in a poker game.

She believed it.

No one could see through *bs* like the Cat.

But he was gone now and they couldn't go on like this forever; they would need supplies soon. Clugot ate. A lot. Where would they get the money to pay for all of it?

She squared her shoulders. She was twenty-one. It was time to take responsibility and face facts. Wildcat might not be coming back.

There had been no message from him at their

prearranged emergency location.

No! He *would* come back. . . as soon as he could. Until then she would do what needed to be done to protect the *Sugarbabe* and its crew!

Heiner interrupted her thoughts.

"The only lead we have at present is that a trader in Port City recalled a suspicious enshrouded traveller asking about exchange rates for miadne and a transport to Slide. A corporation guard remembered seeing this same traveller lurking about the vault buildings earlier in the week. One of our security cameras captured an image of the jewel just before it vanished. That same cloaked traveller is also in several of the background shots at the Corporate Museum where the jewel is permanently housed."

"Where you able to identify anything about this mysterious traveller?"

"No, and we haven't been able to trace the traveller back to our adversary Crisyn either. Big Gun is naturally suspicious of our main competitor."

"Of course."

"Although he cannot accuse them without proof."

"Bad idea, I agree." With some Corporations, even hard evidence wasn't enough. Their lawyers acted like Bizzarro World alchemists, turning gold facts into straw suppositions.

"Arrows, it would probably be best to start your search on Slide."

SpinDrift lifted his mangy head from the floor to whistle a high pitched *tweet*. "Slide, the fabulous pleasure planet?!" He trilled. "I am getting verklempt."

Forget the jewel– the quackhead was thinking of accommodating sex androids for her!

"Oh, no, you don–"

"We'll take the job!" His voice warbled with excitement.

Heiner heard him. "Excellent! Keep me informed as to your progress, Arrows. Time is of the essence. We must have the jewel back before the Day of Ascension."

Lucky did a quick calculation on Minmei. The computer duly responded with its sickeningly upbeat voice.

"THAT WOULD BE THREE EARTH WEEKS FROM TODAY. DON'T BE SAD, MISS LUCKY. LIFE IS JUST A HAILSTORM OF FALLING ROSE PETALS."

What in the hell did that mean? Damn animes and their nonsensical dialogue! Lucky stuck her tongue out at Minmei.

It was not a lot of time to get the job accomplished.

"We'll do our best," Lucky murmured doubtfully to Heiner.

"Wonderful! We'll speak again later. Heiner out."

SpinDrift grabbed Lucky's knees and pulled himself up off the floor. "We're going to the pleasure planet! We're going to the pleeeeassssure planet!"

"Whup-di-do."

SpinDrift put his claws on his. . . well, what passed for his hips. "Oh, show a little spark."

"And just how do we find this peachy planet? Hmm?"

"Hum. Ask Clugot. He'll probably know."

Lucky quirked her brow but stabbed the purple button anyway.

"Urrr?"

"Clugot, do you know the co-ordinates to Slide?"

"Urrr."

Before she could tell the engineer to lay in a course, Clugot had already turned the ship in the direction of the pleasure planet.

Some things just didn't need to be reinforced. Like Spin, Clugot heard the word Slide and lost all reason.

Off they went to find who knew what.

She was sure Wildcat would approve.

After all, this was nothing like the experience on Pittipat.

Nothing like it at all.

EPISODE TWO:
THE FAMILY JEWELS

Cretion, mining and prison outpost

Wildcat Arrows coolly surveyed the dimly lit interior of the tavern.

The murky windows revealed a disreputable bar full of night crawlers. It was exactly what he was looking for.

He immediately slipped inside, into the shadows.

A black satin curtain of waist-length hair slid forward to shield his features from view. Even after months in the dank Cretion mines each strand still glowed like polished ebony. The jet color was rumored to be a gift from an ancient Crow ancestor; chief of his tribe and something of a legend.

As for the sheen. . . well, that was another story.

Several shimmering locks dangled rakishly over his forehead and left eye. And that eye– indeed both eyes– were the most unusual, palest whisper of iced blue. Beguilingly tipped at the corners, they were as clear as the waters of a Loch in spring.

It had often been whispered that the renowned tracker had the sharp focus of an unrelenting warrior.

With good reason.

His remarkable eyes were a gift from two fearless predecessors. The first part of the ancestral hand-me-down originally hailed from a cunning Norse ancestor who was celebrated for having gone a-viking in Caledonia. He finished up his happy journey ensconced in the highlands, blissfully married to a Laird's daughter.

The least said about *that* rogue, the better.

The other part of the genetic boon came from a rather infamous Samurai turned ronin. *He* became Shogun with the grateful help of the Emperor.

It is so fated that such eyes miss nothing.

Arms crossed over his chest, Wildcat leaned back against a stone wall and scanned the room. One leather-clad foot hooked over the other.

Idly, he glanced down at the well-worn moccasins that were laced to just under his knees, halfway up his calves.

'As you explore the path of your life you will find them the finest covering to grace a warrior's foot. . .'

That advice had been given to him long ago and was unquestionably true. In fact, the moccasins had proven themselves this very day for the path he had recently traversed had included a prison break.

He smiled slightly– just a hint of lifting at the corners of lips in a face that had been called utterly sensual, insouciant, and merciless.

His focus was on the room and its inhabitants.

The dank, stale air of the barroom hit his nostrils.

Every Cretion hellhole he had ever been in smelled and looked exactly the same. Musky. Shadowy. Dark. Dangerous.

He did not belong here. Yet, somehow, he felt right at home.

Now what denizens have crawled out from under the Cretion sewers this dark eve? The illicit outpost was a corrupt gathering place for those with special 'creativity'. Usually for obtaining anything that was not– at least at present– corporate controlled. Cretion was welcoming host to thieves, cutthroats, rash entrepreneurs, and erstwhile adventurers.

Wildcat noted that 'welcoming host' applied to anything Cretion was akin to, say, a Venus flytrap lovingly hosting a nice afternoon tea for its parched, winged neighbor.

In a subtle twist of a kind so beloved by the Practitioners of Irony, it just so happened that Cretion was also welcoming host to, *'THE WORST PRISON EVER!'*

Hence the titillating headline in twelve digi-mags this year.

Such a delightful circumstance afforded Cretion management the opportunity for one stop shopping. It was not unheard of for your drinking partner of the evening to roll you over to the authorities for a reward in order to pay for the bar tab on the drinks he had been kindly buying you all night.

Good ol' Cretion cause and effect.

Of course exception to this practice was always taken– which was why at least five knockdown, drag-out fights occurred every night in these happy dens.

Wildcat had never been turned in by "professional courtesy".

He was too good at what he did for that.

And since he was a free agent, no one could be sure what deal they might be stepping on should they happen to cross him at any given time.

Furthermore, he usually made sure his dealings were *fairly* law-abiding. Like Einstein's theory, this viewpoint was relative to whatever laws he happened to be abiding at the time.

Of course, he also tended to favor laws that were most favorable to him.

Hence, *me judice.* I being judge.

Some folks considered that behavior criminal. Others said it was just plain savvy.

Either way, Wildcat had a rep for being on the sharp side of the law. Only he hadn't been too clever this go-around. He was ashamed to admit that he had been bagged in the time-honored manner of all rogues.

He had been caught in bed with the *wrong* woman.

The prison warden's pretty young wife to be exact.

Unfortunately, the warden of Cretion was also the governor of the colony. Not a particularly beneficial coincidence. If Wildcat recalled correctly. . . at the time of discovery the bed frame had been slamming the facts home like an accountant in a budget crunch.

Honestly, he had no idea she was the warden's wife.

He hadn't known she was anybody's *wife*. . . She sure didn't act like anyone's wife!

Of course none of that mattered to the warden, a man whose nickname was *Meanest-Nastiest-Bastard-in-the-Whole-Galaxy* Joe.

Ergo, there had been no trial. No formal sentencing either.

He was sent directly to jail. Do not pass go.

Hard time. Strenuous labor in the dank orzon mines.

Prison is generally a vast warehouse of peculiar oddities, but the strangest curiosity– so far as Wildcat was concerned– was the marvel that the entire cell block had been incarcerated for sleeping with *Meanest-Nastiest-Bastard-in-the-Whole-Galaxy* Joe's pretty lil' wife.

Except. . . no one had actually ridden the "A" train home. So to speak.

No one except him, that is.

Wildcat wasn't altogether sure that entitled him to bragging rights. Considering his current situation and all. And he hadn't had the heart to tell all those other poor schmucks that he had won the "E" ticket. Ride or no, they had still all ended up at the same place– the mines. Her memory was not enough to keep him warm through those cold nights, either.

The warden and his wife had a nice little sideline going for themselves. Orzon was used for ship parts and it was expensive. Consequently, there was a healthy demand for black market orzon.

This made Cretion a real popular watering hole. He had come here on a lead that hadn't panned out. It had turned into quite a trip.

It hadn't taken Wildcat long to figure out that all of the

'special' prisoners had been given dummy idents. Orzon dug up by unregistered prisoners would not have to be turned over to the mining company because there would be no record of the orzon the unregistered prisoners had mined.

Looking on the bright side, Wildcat reasoned that the sour grapes of his labor could be turned into 'wrathade'– if he could escape this hellhole of a planet and refrain from mixing his metaphors.

The sweetest part was that they would never be able to legally track him. Dummy idents meant no prison records.

There weren't a lot of places that he couldn't figure a way out of (or into, for that matter). He had just bided his time until the right way to escape presented itself.

Regrettably, it had taken much longer than he estimated.

Too damn long.

Six stellar months.

On Cretion, prisoners either survived the backbreaking labor or they didn't. Their choice. Wildcat's tall, muscular frame– another ancestral gift from the powerful Scottish Laird of the highlands– had helped him endure the strenuous labor.

But even he could only take so much.

He needed a way off this dung heap. *Fast.*

A line briefly formed in the middle of his smooth forehead as he sized up a potential mark. A Zoltarian captain.

Probably pirate.

She was sitting at a table, surrounded by her crew. Snorting in laughter to the male on her left, she snatched a tankard skin off the rickety bar tray. In an instant, long, pointed fangs pierced the bladder of Cretion hootch.

Down the hatch it went. *Glub, glub, glub.*

While this was going on, the comrade to her right spit three times, then brayed out cusses, sounding exactly like an ass with turrets. He followed up nicely on this set by keeling backwards right over his chair.

Face up, he flopped across the floor and might well have been taken for dead if not for the faint, intermittent twitching in the vicinity of his groin and the occasional hee-haw sound coming from his mouth.

Wildcat cocked his head to the side with a kind of horrified fascination as he watched the floor show. *No mystery now as to why Zoltarians have a real hard time scoring in bars. . .*

He winced as the captain cracked open a hard-shelled *jub-jub* by using the poor lout's forehead as a nutcracker.

Ouch. *That'll hurt in the morning.*

The pirate's brethren did not appear to notice their mate's semi-demise. By their raucous behavior, the scruffy band had been on the sauce for hours.

Hell, maybe they'd been drinking for days.

With Zoltarians, you never knew.

Their aggressive in your face attitude was only surpassed by their unending capacity for high octane rotgut. Cretion grog fit that bill perfectly. Big punch, little price.

The captain suddenly noticed him by the door and arched her slanted brows in interest.

Oh, hell no.

Wildcat closed his eyes and exhaled as he tried to talk

sense to himself. He was stranded on this planet and if he didn't get out of here soon, there was a real possibility that his bed tonight– and every night *forever*– was going to be the stone floor of a six by eight foot cell.

If he was lucky.

They could decide to just kill him as a thank you for the trouble he caused. This pirate captain might be his only chance.

He cringed. Damn, but he really, *really* hated that thing they did with their teeth!

Zoltarian? Only as a last resort.

For the time being, he decided to ignore her blatant invitation.

He carefully continued his survey of the murky barroom. In one corner, a Kneph was sketching on the wall with some kind of root vegetable. She loudly extolled the virtues of soup.

He crossed his eyes.

There was no way he was going to wrangle with a Kneph. They were dubbed *'naggers of the known universe'* for good reason. Six co-dependent personalities. All migraine inducing.

Wildcat recoiled as he imagined those six distinct female voices demanding he pick up the pace. *No, slow down. . .* Harder!. . . *Deeper. . .* Stop. . . *Go. . .* Pu-u-u-ussssh!

Hell no.

He didn't mind working up a proper sweat for the right cause, but he had never been known as one that did what was demanded of him. Undoubtedly, the Kneph would soon find him more than she bargained for. And one of those irksome personalities might alert the authorities.

Without hesitation, he moved on.

Towards the back of the room, a nasty batch of Taman mercenaries were live-hunting a late snack. As Wildcat watched, the server released the trap door on a cage of *snurts*.

The furry, black beasties scurried across the stone floor in a flurry of feathers and shrieks.

But it was too late for them.

Like a hailstorm of lightening arrows, seven Taman laz-lances zinged through the air. They homed in on their targets, efficiently snuffing and toasting the poor critters in one streamlined maneuver.

With a cool flick of Taman talons, the laz-lances were retrieved and the unfortunate snurts were served up en brochette.

Cretion blue plate special.

The sight made Wildcat slightly nauseous.

It had been a long while since he had last eaten; nevertheless, his Earthboy sensibilities were not yet honed to sizzled snurt. Oh, he supposed he had ingested worse in his lifetime– but he wasn't too keen to test that supposition out, thank you very much.

No one else was in the bar.

Wildcat's focus drifted reluctantly back to the Zoltarian. If one of the Taman mercs had been female, he might well have been on his way to his first taste of Kentucky Fried Snurt.

But that wasn't the case.

The pirate captain was his only chance. She had what

he needed: an airship. He could not be seen on the streets again. The *sniffers* were closing in on him fast; he needed to act now.

He wasn't just itchin' to get off this planet; he was hankerin' to get at something else.

Before he had escaped he had heard a rumor in the mines.

Word in the gulag was that the Heart of the Merchandiser had been lifted.

Wildcat knew that if there was one thing prisoners usually got right, it was the current state of happenings in the woo-woo world of criminal hijinks. As they say on the ol'homeball, that lil' information highway flowed freely three sixty-five twenty-four seven. And amen to that.

Ah, miadne. . .

The one substance that could fuel a galaxy-wide circle jerk amongst bandits everywhere. *Beautiful miadne!* It was the main standard behind every currency in the galaxy. And the Heart of the Merchandiser was the largest single chunk of inclusion-free miadne known to exist in the universe.

Wildcat touched his heart and bowed his head in mock homage.

Truth was, Wildcat Arrows had a rep for finding things. Oil. Lost loves. Codes. Secret admirers. You name it; *he* could track it. Of all the things the Cat could find– well, he was simply the best at locating lost 'jewels'.

One could almost say he devoted his life to it.

Funny how that life had turned out. . .

It hadn't been all that long ago that Earth had been

introduced to Tamans, Cretions, Snurts, and a plethora of extraterrestrial surprises that had just been waiting to go '*bugga-bugga!*' to Earthlings.

In a Klein bottle twist, decades of Hollywood foreshadowing about the scourge of alien contact– imax movies of bug-eyed monsters munching Aunt Sue's brain– books preaching a tentacled apocalypse– dire cookbooks with recipes of stir-fried man– never came to pass.

We had seen the enemy and it was us.

Contact came in the form of a simple corporate takeover.

It seemed a mark, a yen, a buck, or a pound made ze universe go round. Earth was invited (absorbed) into the Consortium of Corporate Systems, or Concorp for short.

Nothing adapted as well as a businessman sniffing streaming money on the solar wind. All xenophobia was quickly caste aside in the name of golden opportunity.

The entire galaxy was one big corporate party, *brotha.*[2]

Earthlings had shown a potential aptitude for making money for the galactic corporations.

Oh, and Earth had macadamia nuts.

The highly prized seed turned out to be the planet's *only* redeemable export. Mankind's true claim to universal recognition had been embedded in a Sausalito cookie for decades. Who knew?

---

[2] Off Earth went into the wild blue dot Milky Way com to be welcomed into the Nasdaq of galactic worlds. And they were welcomed by these sentient businessmen. But not because of their scientific achievements. ***"Big Deal."*** had been the general response to that. Nor were they welcomed for their enlightened progression up the evolutionary ladder. ***("So what? You can lead a Vrek to sludge but can you make him paddle?")*** Or their literature. ***("Feh.")*** Or their art. ***("Been there, drew that.")*** Or because of their beautiful uniqueness in the universal tank of intelligent life. ***("You're killing us here.")*** No, they were welcomed because they knew the value of cutting a deal. Moreover, they knew to charge interest for the pleasure of being cut in on that deal. And that, my friends, is potential.

Stock prices on macadamia commodities soared.

Since 2014 e.t., Earth had been part of Concorp's entry level up-and-comers. As the new toys on the block, Earthlings became a galactic cause célèbre. Sought after for exciting, energetic copulation and not much else.

The musings of pulp science fiction writers of the past turned out to be accurate. Advanced species really were interested in hot sex with the people from Earth.

As luck would have it, Wildcat Arrows was one of the most intriguing of the Earth breeds. Hell-raisin'. Hard-lovin'. Wild-ridin'. He was a rogue who lived for danger, high stakes, and the thrill of the game.

And best of all, he could make love like there was no tomorrow.

An expert at giving satisfaction but not his heart.

Never his heart.

Attracted to these males' fiery dispositions, extra-terrestrial females had a name for such men. They called them *'chain lightning'*.

But never to their faces.

Wildcat knew this and was not above using it to his advantage– if he had to. Resolved, he squared shoulders that had become much broader since his forced servitude in the mines. Whatever he had to do to leave here, he'd do.

His one hope was that Lucky and that pea-brained SpinDrift had the good sense to dry-dock the *Sugarbabe* and hole up at Mama Bros Almost Used Emporium and Garage.

The last thing he wanted to do was chase around the galaxy after them. Every tracker, thief, purveyor of unusual artifacts and their accompanying squads of goon opportunists would be after that miadne!

He didn't want to lose any time in tracking it.

That jewel was a key to the sweet life.

He only hoped they hadn't been foolish enough to be suckered into something stupid while he was away.

He closed his eyes. A vision of Lucky's trusting innocence and SpinDrift's brainless expression crossed his mind. Add to that vision Clugot– whose name should have been Clueless– and you had the perfect recipe for trouble a la mode.

Oh hell. He needed to get back to his ship pronto.

Wildcat ground his teeth as made his way to the Zoltarian's table. With no money, no credit, no miadne, no papers, and no transport, he was going to have to do whatever it took to get back to them. He had vowed to protect Lucky and that was one promise he intended to keep.

Several of the Zoltarian's shipmates growled as he approached, but the captain snapped her teeth at them and they quickly shrank back into their pursuit of drink.

"Sit here, Earthman." She patted the seat next to her with fingers that sported remarkably long nails. The manicured set had been done in the french style. Tiny sparkling diamonds were delicately set into each pointed nail tip.

Wildcat had almost convinced himself that the little Asian manicure shop at the end of the street had been a figment of his imagination. While he had stealthily crept by the windows, he had caught a glimpse of a blobish alien having what he assumed was a pedicure. Several diligent manicurists attended the client as her tentacles stretched across several stools. While he had stopped to stare, bright crimson nail polish and tiny white hearts were applied to the end of each tentacle.

Wildcat's eyes had crossed.

Once contact had been made, it hadn't taken long for the nail shops to launch themselves into space. Just like on Earth, they cropped up everywhere.

He took a seat and the Zoltarian graciously offered him a swig of her tankard bladder.

The thought of where that bladder had originated made him hold up his hand to politely decline.

She laughed. "Earthlings are so conventional, so provincial. I find most are afraid to partake of new experiences." She leaned closer to him. "You will never learn if you do not *experience*, my friend." She winked at him.

Truth was, Wildcat had partaken of more new experiences in his lifetime than this Zoltarian woman would ever imagine.

A line of amusement curved his cheek, but he played the role she asked of him.

"Perhaps you could show me?"

The Zoltarian chuckled. "Perhaps. Perhaps. You Earthmen are still quite the novelty. A new flavor to us. Still, I don't wish to upset your fragile sensibilities; I was a bit too much for the last one of your kind that I. . . encountered." Her tongue licked over her incisors suggestively.

Wildcat tried to hide his shudder of revulsion. He

really hated that thing they did with their teeth!

Think of Lucky.

He kept repeating that to himself as he set his focus only on her. Long shimmering black lashes shielded his eyes; flickering glints of azure flashed through the dark crescents.

Better to let her wonder what he was thinking. He was having a hard time committing to this.

The Zoltarian sucked in her breath. "I have never seen hair that glistens so. You are utterly beautiful, my friend. Did you know that?"

He didn't. And he had never much cared one way or the other. But he knew what he had to do. If he didn't focus on what Zoltarians did with their teeth, he would be fine.

"I could arrange for you to feel my hair sliding over you." He purred as he gave her a slow smile. "Perhaps you will *glisten* too," he whispered.

It worked. She threw back her head and roared with laughter. "I like you. Come, let us go."

His eyes narrowed. Caution was the rule in these places. "Where?"

"To my ship, of course. I have a nice private cabin; we won't be disturbed."

She started to rise, assuming that the deal was sealed. Wildcat's hand shot out and grabbed her wrist, forestalling her.

"There is one condition."

She looked cooly down at his firm hold on her wrist. Her nostrils flared with annoyance. "There usually is. What do you want?"

He was walking a thin line and he knew it; she was his only ticket out. Still, he held his ground. "I remain on your ship when you leave Cretion orbit. Let's just say I need transport."

The Zoltarian's crimson eyes gleamed with something Wildcat did not like. "I see. You know there have been rumors of a prisoner who escaped from the mines. That prisoner wouldn't be you, would it?"

Wildcat studied her face carefully before responding. If she didn't like his answer, she would turn him in. On the other hand, Zoltarians were known for adopting instant loyalty to those they took a liking to. They always reminded him of faithful pups, even though they were definitely humanoid, had no fur, and could never be made to chase a stick.

"Couldn't be me," he drawled. "I was home fantasizing about Zoltarian women all day."

She snorted, leaning closer to examine his features. Even in the darkened room, his exotic looks were positively arresting.

And those astonishing eyes!

Zoltarians considered that particular shade of blue matchless. His eyes were most erotic. A sensual glance from them were as potent as a touch. And they had the strangest calming effect. . .

They almost whispered to her: *Trust me.*

She didn't hesitate.

"You have a bargain, Earthling. Where do you wish passage to?"

"Any port but here, Captain."

She nodded. "Come with me, then, but be forewarned; I intend to get the full fare out of you."

He flashed her a rakish grin. "I'd never give half."

She warmed up to his charm. "What is your name, my alluring wanderer?"

"Jack."

" I hear those of your world have two designations. Your other name? "

"Hammer."

"Good. Come, Jack Hammer."

She rose and headed to the door.

"That's almost poetic," Wildcat murmured aloud, even though there was no one around him to enjoy the joke.

A soft, faint susurration floated around him; an invisible whisper on the air like a feather gently tickling.

Wildcat arched his brow, then gazed with full intent into the shadows behind him.

"Are you coming?" the Zoltarian asked impatiently.

"Undoubtedly, madam." He strolled after the pirate.

As he approached her ship he realized, in an almost zen-like moment, that Zoltarian space travel would be much like eskrima fighting. Fast, hard-hitting, and highly combative.

He glanced at the statuesque captain.

She was actually very alluring. It had been a while; but he was up for a dynamic match.

No doubt he would get it from her.

EPISODE THREE:
WHO GOES THERE

Planet Slide, The Lost Without Your Love Playhouse

Two hulking guards were blocking the entrance to a corridor.

Which was odd in a pleasure house.

The idea was to get someone inside, not keep them out.

Kerreth flattened himself against a wall and covertly watched the guards. Someone down the other end of that hallway had *something* that needed guarding and they were willing to pay big for the extra detailing to do it.

He was close.

He could almost feel that perfect wad of miadne cooling off his palm. *Come to me, my lovely Heart of the Merchandiser.*

He could not believe his good fortune when the call came about the missing jewel. He had the best informers that money and threats could buy. It goes to show that quality always pays off.

There was never a substitute for a first class snitch.

The fuzzy trail had led to this backburner pleasure planet. Kerreth had apparently beaten the pack to it.

Feels good, too.

There was no way he was going to let that prize out of his grasp. And as soon as he had it, he was out of here faster than you could say 'wham, bam, thank you for the glam'.

Got to love that Earth Slang.

The guards were about to round the corner.

Silently, Kerreth inched along the passageway. Up ahead, indented in the wall, was a portal frame. He needed to reach it before those lugnuts turned into the hallway and caught him.

Just as the guards' shadows lengthened along the corridor up ahead, Kerreth slid into the recessed area. The doors automatically rolled open allowing him to duck inside, out of sight. They closed silently behind him.

He found himself in a small storeroom.

Plenty to use in here, he realized as he looked around the tiny room. *Let's see. . . clothing, food packs, water, health boost bars. Everything that is needed for the perfect caper and getaway. Smart. Real smart.*

One day he intended to write a manual on how to heist-proof one's base of operations. The first step would be to *not* leave extra uniforms and supplies around that would allow one's infiltrators and/or enemies to complete their missions.

A grin spread across his face. Thankfully, these geniuses hadn't gotten the memo. *Health boost bars, for suck's sake!*

Fuel your attacker, why don't you? He shook his head.

After removing his micro tool kit, he pulled one of the

waiter's uniforms off the rack in front of him, threw off his own clothes, and slipped into it.

To be safe, he kicked his own clothes to the back of a bottom shelf of a cubby to his left. Way out of sight.

He was just reaching for his Linkpod when the doors behind him suddenly opened.

Two meaty guards stared suspiciously at him.

They didn't seem like the giggle and go types.

"You there! What are you doing in here? This is a sealed off area!"

Kerreth was nothing if not quick. "I was sent here to inventory the clothing supply."

"Well, move it along! We have orders to lock down this entire corridor. Some honcha has paid the Boss plenty for privacy."

"Privacy?" Not the usual request in one of these houses.

The guard became strangely defensive of his task. "It's not like it hasn't happened before. Remember, what occurs on Slide is never suspect on Slide. You shouldn't be questioning that."

Another corporate flunky. The lugnut had actually milked *and* swallowed the propaganda. *Idiot.* "Yeah. Sure."

Kerreth glanced discreetly over his shoulder. He needed to retrieve that Linkpod on his belt; he had only intended to put it down for a few moments while he was changing. Bad timing.

"Fine. I'll just finish up in here and then leave as you requested."

"It wasn't a request. You're going. *Now.*" The guards motioned him through the doors with their weapons.

There was nothing Kerreth could do.

He was forced to leave his Linkpod behind.

The lesson was not lost on him: *Whenever a person starts feeling good about his chances, the Law of Beat Down always catches up to slap him upside the head.*

He would have to try to retrieve it again later.

That is, if he ever wanted to get off this planet and back to his so-called ride home. That Linkpod was his only connection to it and that 'ride' was not going to wait long. The disreputable team of bounty hunters he had hired to transport him here and back would not hang around should he miss the rendezvous point. They would happily ditch him and be out after their next bounty.

The guard sealed the door with a shutdown lock.

Flickerin' goofs. That was going to be very difficult if not impossible to crack.

"Back to your madam!"

Before they moved off down the passage they shoved him in the direction of the nexus artery where the bawdyhouse business partners had their offices.

My madam? Kerreth frowned. *Well, the uniform is a bit. . . silky.*

Hmmm.

No choice but to find another way in. He headed off in the opposite direction. As he rounded the next corridor, he overheard two beings talking in the hallway.

Bickering would be more like it.

They were coming from the other side of that blocked off corridor. His ears perked up when the words 'miadne' and 'Heart of the Merchandiser' were bandied about. . .

* * *

"What do you make of that, Spin?"

Lucky rubbed the side of her neck as she walked back down the aisle toward the front gates. SpinDrift waddled along beside her.

"Well, if anyone was ever in that room, they have long since departed. Nothing was in there to speak of. Not even a whiff of a clue!" SpinDrift pursed his beak into a moue.

Which looked very funny on a Floop.

Lucky giggled.

"What is so amusing?"

"Nothing."

"Hmf! No miadne. No Heart of the Merchandiser. In fact, everything was so perfect in that room, you'd think that it was a set design or something."

"It was a set design. Little Bo Peep, I think. But I agree; it was a little too perfect." Lucky plucked one of Spin's molted feathers off her arm and tossed it to the floor. "Except for that oddly cracked vase. . ."

"You mean this one?" The Floop reached inside his motley coat to one of his hidden pockets and pulled out the piece of pottery in question.

Lucky gasped. *"You lifted it?!* Whatever for? Good grief! We could be detained for stealing! What were you thinking?! You know these pleasure palaces have the strictest rules! Wildcat's friend, Juko, was sent to a frozen gulag for three years just for taking a towel. *A towel, for flickerin's sake!!"*

"Oh, hush it. It's not like they can do anything with it. See, it's too cracked."

"Then what do you want with it?"

"Well, I thought a little glue might–"

The vase slipped from his claw onto the floor. It smashed into 5,835,774 pieces.

"Oh, dear."

"Brilliant! Look what you– " she stopped short. "Wait, Spin. . . what's that?" Lucky pointed to a small button-like object lying in the middle of the fragments.

"It must have been inside the vase." SpinDrift bent over to investigate, his feathered butt bouncing in the air.

Three visiting Kneph's happened to be passing by the intersecting corridor. They all snarled in interest.[3]

SpinDrift curled his beak at them. "Don't you wish!" He clucked his tongue. "Rude rubes. Timing is *everything*, Lucky. Just remember that."

"Forget about them, Spin. What is that thing?"

"Looks like some sort of chip. Maybe we should take it back to the ship to check it out?"

"Do you think someone left us a clue about the stolen miadne?"

"It's possible, but unlikely."

"Do you think Minmei can decipher it?"

"It's possible, but unlikely."

"Mmm." Lucky noticed a sleek male android knock on a door, then enter a room. No need to guess why.

This was the Lost Without Your Love playhouse.

---

[3] Despite Floops ongoing disregard of all things Kneph, Knephs were always infatuated with Floops. It was a subject often chuckled over at corporate water fountains.

She tried not to wheeze.

Okay, so she wasn't sure she approved– but how did they make those guys so perfect looking?

SpinDrift noticed her line of sight. His round eyes widened as his crockpot brain slowly stewed out an idea.

"You know, Lucky, we don't have to get right back to the ship. . . You could take some r and r. Experiment with the local fauna, as they say." He fluttered his lashes in a silly attempt at looking lascivious.

Lucky scoffed. "Who actually says that, Spin?"

"They say it. Everyone knows *they*! But you're trying to change the subject– what do *you* say?"

"I say, no thank you."

SpinDrift clucked an expletive of dismay. In Floopese. *"Brwwuuk!"*

"Look, I don't want some quasi male machine thing pawing at me! I'd rather– *omph!"*

They had just rounded the corner and Lucky had apparently walked into a solid wall of *hard.*

Dazed, she looked up into a gorgeous, masculine face.

He was delicious.

Perfectly sculpted lips, firm, yet sensual– they dared one to get closer. Straight, aquiline nose. Golden, expressive eyes that were deep set and beautifully shaped.

They reminded Lucky of rich, shimmering metal. She had heard such a color described once in an Earth broadcast as *El Dorado gold.*

It sure fit him, because he looked like a treasure chest for that special woman lucky enough to unlock his interest.

To complete the roguish image, the man's bronzed skin

was the warm color of creamed coffee. He looked as if he had been standing in the sun on the deck of an old sailing ship for most of his life. His hair, which fell in tousled cascades to the base of his neck, seemed to be a combination of sun-streaked mocha and gold. The attractive ruffled strands reminded Lucky of the variegated colors of Earth that she secretly missed.

Basically, standing before her was a prize wrapped up in the form of a man. And every superlative detail enticed a woman to go after it.

Or, in this case, hunt down the 'booty'.

The illusion of handsome, swaggering 'scalawag' was flawless.

Lucky's amazed gaze travelled down the brawny chest, noting the fitted jumpsuit. It was the uniform of a male servicer.

And, my-oh-my, was it tight!

In fact, the uniform was so snug that her eyes were pulled– totally against their will of course– to the overstuffed crotch.

Her pupils dilated considerably.

The impressive bulge was a proud display.

Lucky could not tear her eyes away from it. *Good gawd. It's some sort of fiendish chubby magnet!*

When she finally broke her fixated stare away from the package, she came face-to-face with a demure disclosure. His identification was embroidered over the chest pocket of the jumpsuit. *Slick Slowhand.*

"Holy cannoli." She whistled.

So this was a pleasure android. Lucky had heard the

stories, of course, but she had never seen one for herself.

My-oh-my.

Just looking at him made her toes curl.

"You were saying?" SpinDrift nudged her.

"He *is* something, isn't he?"

"Word."

"Why do you think they make them so unrealistically beautiful, Spin?"

"It's like he's too good to be true!" Floops loved looking at humans. They considered them all pretty works of art. Go figure.

Lucky stood on tiptoes. Bringing herself right up into the android's face. She stared directly into his deep-set eyes.

"His features are incredibly sexy. . ." She glanced over her shoulder at SpinDrift. "Nobody ever looks this perfect."

Kerreth stared back at the woman, momentarily speechless. *What was she talking about?* He had never paid much attention to his appearance– but something about it sure seemed to please her.

SpinDrift shrugged. "Oh, I don't know; he looks pretty realistic to me. . ."

"Really?" Lucky quirked an eyebrow. "And what about this?" She reached down and cupped his manhood.

Kerreth's mouth dropped open.

He slowly glanced down to see this stranger's hand cupping his privates. Stupefied, he watched as she hefted the weighty bundle up and down. *Twice.*

She snorted. "Right. *As if.*"

SpinDrift crossed his arms over his chest. "They do say

they are a hard act to follow. Pun intended."

"Look, no real man is built like that. It's preposterous."

Completely astonished, Kerreth gaped at this strange woman, who– one might say– had him right in the palm of her hand. She was rather. . . pretty.

Lucky suddenly felt the cozy bundle twitch to life.

She yanked her hand back, quick.

Kerreth thought it wise to remain silent for the time being.

Meanwhile, SpinDrift was still agog at the whole idea of Lucky taking advantage of the opportunity– it being his personal opinion that she was long overdue. Floops loved getting excited for their friends; they considered it their job and their mission.

"Well, I think this speaks for itself, Spin It's not my cuppa."

The Floop had other ideas. His eyes moistened as he clasped his claws together in sublime joy. "Oh, Lucky, this is the one!! I know it!"

"Respect." But Lucky continued to gawk at the unusual specimen. She simply could not take her eyes off him. "Know what I mean, Spin? R-e-s-p-e-c-t."

"Come on, do give him a try, Lucky! How can you not? Just *look* at him!" SpinDrift's cajoling brought her back down to Slide firma.

No matter how many times she tried to educate SpinDrift on the relationship between male and female Earthlings, she more than suspected that she had set the bar too high.

The Floop just didn't get it.

Yes, sex was good and all (at least that is what she was led to believe, having no personal experience in the area); but preferably there was more to it than just the boinking.

Besides, all those wonky relationship variables usually spelled trouble of some kind. Look at Wildcat; he was always getting into hot water over women. It wouldn't be nearly so bad if the rascal didn't always dive head first into it!

She sighed. "Don't be ridiculous, Spin. Think of the complications."

"What complications? He's an android. That's. The. Beauty. Of. It." The Floop enunciated each word slowly in order to allow his theory to sink in.

As if he had just discovered Plan 9.

"After all this time, you can quench that thirst, Lucky Red Arrows." He pointed a spindly claw straight at the android. "This is your font. Drink, girl! Drink!"

Kerreth, who had been listening to this bizarre conversation, stared down at the insane duo with narrowed eyes. *Why was everyone suddenly mistaking him for a flickerin' pleasure droid?* First the guards, now these two.

The one that had bumped into him was rather engaging, he had to admit. She appeared to be a human female with really nice green eyes.

Like him, she used a lot of Earth slang.

But the other one– the one who was gawking at him like he might be some sort of meal for his companion– looked like he suffered from a bad case of the stupids.

As he observed the Floop, Kerreth had the distinct impression that the star might be illuminated . . . but there was no fusion going on.

Beyond belief, the redheaded female notched her chin up and proceeded to admonish him.

"You should pay more attention to where you are going. You almost injured me."

"Excuse me?" It was not a request for pardon. Kerreth's "perfect" features turned to stone. "I should watch where *I'm* going?"

"Exactly. Pay attention to your courtesy programming."

"My what?

"Now step aside! We need to pass; we have no time for this."

SpinDrift moaned sadly. He was seeing all his hopes and dreams flutter away. "I can't believe you're going to let this golden-haired opportunity get by you, Lucky. Where have I gone wrong with you?"

Lucky snorted. "Really, Spin; I don't think he is all that."

SpinDrift snorted back.

"I'm serious; I've seen better. We can *do* better. Let's go."

Kerreth's nostrils flared. First, the woman rudely dissects him, then she insults and dismisses him. *I don't think so, green eyes.* And why was the annoying one steering her to. . . *what?* Try him out? Sure, the girl was pretty– real pretty– but a tad outlandish; even for his tastes.

He wondered if all the women on her home world greeted men by grabbing their sacks and weighing them out to see if they passed muster. Truly weird.

Kerreth was seriously considering knocking their heads together when Lucky went on to utter the magic words:

"Besides,"– she chatted to her friend as if he hadn't spoken at all– "we need to find that Heart of the Merchandiser."

Hmmm, so they were after the jewel, too.

Kerreth paused to reconsider his next move.

"In case you've forgotten," Lucky frowned at SpinDrift, "we are on a mission here. The trail is growing cold while we waste time ogling this mechanical putz."

That did it.

Kerreth decided payback would be forthcoming. Now, later, didn't matter to him. But it was on its way.

So, they were either on a mission to find the miadne for themselves or they were working for someone else. . .

The later possibility was the most troubling. If they were here at the behest of someone else, who sent them? And what was their connection to that stone? He needed to find out. That jewel belonged to him and he had no intention of sharing.

Kerreth watched them intently from under hooded eyes.

He had overheard some of their conversation just before the woman had slammed into him. It wasn't hard to put two and two together. The feathery one had called her *Arrows*.

She must be tied somehow to that famous tracker.

Kerreth viewed her askance. Wildcat Arrows was not only a rebel, but an exceedingly shrewd dealer in matters of bartering. Rumor had it he often dealt with pirates and other unsavory characters. Some said he was a pirate himself.

Did Arrows send her? Was she his wife? She could be his lover– sent in as a shill. No telling.

Only, the woman in front of him appeared to be almost naive.

Couldn't be. Not hanging out with that scalawag.

The whole thing didn't jive. *Must be an ac*t. Had to be.

He cocked his head to the side as he studied her. Her thick, curly hair had been tied back in a loose ponytail. Her lips were full and very sweet-looking. Lush and pink and. . .

His hardened rogue's heart took a double-beat.

What the. . .?

Lucky suddenly lifted her hand and pushed a few tendrils of hair off his face.

Thumpthump. Thumpthump.

Underlying his traitorous blood pressure, Kerreth discovered he was dumbfounded. Did this woman actually believe he was a flickerin' pleasure droid?

Despite the advances in robotic technology, androids were still not coming across as real. Yet, these two not only believed it, the feathered one was trying to convince the woman to give him a test drive.

He tried not to grin.

This is really too priceless to pass by. Take advantage of it, he told himself. *Take advantage.*

In the next instant, he devised his plan.

Which basically boiled down to a short list with a 'gotta do' at the end.

He was stuck on Slide as long as he couldn't get to his Linkpod. It was clear he couldn't get to his Linkpod as long as that flickerin' door remained sealed and guarded by the two happy lugnuts. And the longer he cooled here. . . the cooler the trail to the treasure.

These two brainpuddings were also hunting the miadne jewel and had, possibly, against all odds, beaten him to a lead.

Moreover, they appeared to have the *only* lead.

By their own accounts, the room had been left pristine; the only thing out of place had been that cracked (and now smashed) jug.

Something had been in that vase. . .

He needed to find out what they uncovered.

In order to do that, there was only one thing for him to do: be the uber-pleasure machine they both believed him to be.

He purposely blinked his eyes a few times and flashed her a smile so utterly sexual that there was no way it could be misinterpreted. Even by her.

He poured wickedness all over it.

"My apologies, mistress. Your. . . er, lush. . . sweetness overwhelmed my normal sense of coordination."

"My lush sweetness?"

Instead of becoming clay at his feet, she laughed right in his face. "Boy, oh boy, they program you to really lay it on thick, don't they?"

"You have no idea," he murmured in a low tone.

At the sound of such a deep, sexy voice, Lucky mirrored her other name by turned bright red. Her breath caught in her throat.

That voice was awfully good! It rolled over a girl like smooth, rich chocolate. She analyzed the destructive power of the accompanying dimples. High level of kill, to be sure.

How did they get robots to be this sexy anyway?

Gawd, he was drool-i-licious!

She was positive most women won't mind in the least if he had to keep it going with WD4O. As long as the hunk kept it going.

SpinDrift tweeted a kind of breathless whistle as he viewed the exchange. The pervert!

"All-all right. Apology accepted." Embarrassed, Lucky made to push past the squire of active hit programming on the move.

"Wait."

Her footstep faltered and she pivoted slightly.

Their eyes locked.

In that instant, Kerreth thought: *I've got her.*

While Lucky firmly thought: *It's sayonara for you, robo boy.*

"Are you leaving Slide now?"

"Yes."

"Take me with you."

"Brwaak!" The Floop almost molted right there.

Lucky threw Spin a dirty look before focusing back to the artificial Casanova. "Why would I do that?"

"I wish to leave this place."

"That's impossible. You are basically a machine and-"

"Not simply a machine." A proud glint formed in his eye. He stood taller as he boastfully announced, "I am the Masterstroke 5000."

"Braaaaaaaawk!" This time, Spin did molt. Half of his coat just fell off him and dumped onto the floor.

Lucky didn't know what to look at first. Her half-bald companion or the oversexed sex machine standing in front of her. *"You're a wha?"*

Kerreth arched his brow with feigned self-importance and tried not to laugh. "A Masterstroke 6000."

"I thought you just said 5000."

"Yes. As we were speaking, my programming was instantly upgraded via downlink. I am now even more improved."

"How. . . *What?"*

"Instead of stopping between bouts of lovemaking, I am now able to continue for up to five sessions without taking any time to recharge my thrusters."

"Good gawd." Lucky stared at him in fascinated horror.

Spin gave up and just fell to the floor on top of his shed feathers.

Kerreth inclined his head in a slight bow.

"A Masterstroke 6000!" Spin managed to lift his head up off the ground. "I heard they were lifelike, Lucky, but I never–! He's a masterpiece!!"

Lucky starred at the strapping robot in awe. "Oh, the humanity."

"Oh, the testosterone!" Spin squawked, then collapsed again.

Lucky put her hands on her hips and shook her head to clear it. "Are you through with us?"

"No."

"I was afraid of that."

"You see, the Masterstroke 5, er, 6000 is different from any of its predecessors. To increase my functioning, my creator imbued my programming with a curiosity of all things. In sexual situations, this curiosity allows me to create more of a craving in women."

Lucky covered her ears. "I don't want to hear this."

"I can create a ravenous desire with the touch of my–"

"La-la-la-la."

Kerreth stood in front of her and gently clasped her wrists, taking her hands down.

His touch was warm and soothing. In fact, it had a strong emulation of life force to it. A good feel.

Part of the realistic programming, Lucky supposed.

The fact that this robot was observing her from under lowered lids unnerved her slightly. Robots shouldn't seem this hunky. Or this sensual.

She might have blushed under his regard– until a line of amusement curled his beautiful, smug lips.

What a tool.

"I can assure you, my programming goes well beyond anything you can imagine," he whispered in a silky, bedroom voice.

Not. Playing. Fair. A light sheen of sweat dotted Lucky's forehead. How could a stupid machine unnerve her?

There was something totally intimidating about being in this android's crosshairs. It was as if his designers had invented a working recipe for all of the traits she secretly fantasized about and then they went and cooked him up, nice and perfect.

It wasn't right!

They seemed to have produced a work of art that she just

had to taste–

No wonder women blew fortunes to come to these posh resorts! Stupid pleasure palaces.

Lucky tried to ignore the sexual wave attack by concentrating on what robo boy was saying.

". . .as a special experimental prototype, I was also given the ability to choose my methods of satisfaction."

"*Special prototype?* What does that mean, Spin?

"Never mind that. Find out about all those methods of satisfaction!" Spin croaked back to her. "Please observe all that first-rate equipment and come to your senses, Lucky-girl."

Lucky coughed. Her expressive eyes threw a warning to the happy-go-lucky Floop. They said: *Stop. Right now. If not, I will either kill you or burst out laughing – and then kill you.*

SpinDrift *fnurr-fnurred.*

The android continued talking as if none of this was going on in front of him.

". . . because of this, I have begun to grow weary of servicing so many females."

"That is a chore, isn't it?" Lucky stretched her arms and yawned.

"I am overwhelmed with the task load."

She shook her head as if she were agreeing with the cross-wired twit. "An android as fine as you must be a very busy boy-droid."

"He gives a deeper meaning to the term; remember that." Spin pulled himself up off the floor.

Lucky rolled her eyes.

"On the bad days I lose count, mistress." His impossibly beautiful eyes gleamed mischievously under impossibly long lashes.

"Poor dear. How many do you have to 'do' on average?" Lucky was being bad, but this misfiring doof really asked for it.

"I am– *excuse me*?"

"How many women do you have to service at one time? Or. . ." She tapped her finger on her lip. "Is it just women?"

Kerreth's mouth dropped opened but nothing came out.

"Come now, an android– especially a pleasure android– should not be shy."

He seemed to bristle "I am strictly designed for women," he responded flatly.

"Of course you are."

Kerreth squinted at her, clearly not liking her reply.

What a riot.

"So, how many women are we talking about? That massive number that you 'grow so weary of'?"

Kerreth blinked. Twice. How had the conversation devolved into this? What kind of range *did* a pleasure droid have any way? He scratched his arm.

Perhaps they hit a stride and went with it?

Or. . . maybe they kind of levelled up? Lucky mongrels.

He'd better say something before she got suspicious. "I can assure you that you would tire out long before I do."

SpinDrift took offense at that assessment. After all, Lucky was his best friend in all the galaxies! The android's statement hinted at an insult.

SpinDrift crossed his wiry arms. "Hmf! I'll have you

know my Lucky is the most active female in twenty-six quadrants!"

Lucky coughed.

Kerreth quirked his brow and regarded the woman in a new, interested light. "Is that so?" he drawled.

"You are not helping me here." Lucky cleared her throat. "Ahem. Are you sure this desire you have to explore is not a design flaw? You may have a glitch in your program or even a *No-No-Nanite* virus."

"Wasn't that a play on Robot Theater 3K? I'm sure of it, Lucky. . . it was an all droid revue and– *ouch!*"

Lucky kicked Spin. "Shush!"

Kerreth, realizing that he was in the presence of two spaceheads, decided to move the conversation along in the direction he needed it to go.

He didn't care what he had to say– he was getting on their ship.

"I do wish to explore new experiences, naturally. You will find me an enjoyable and gifted experience." He gazed down at her and winked lazily. "I will make it so for you."

The most beautiful looking male to ever proposition her and he had several gears loose! Literally. Yeah, sure, she needed a whackjob pleasure droid getting underfoot. . .

Like she needed a dose of *buggeritis type II!*

Why do things like this always happen to her?

If they didn't have to leave Slide quickly, this actually would have been amusing. The android was almost winning her over with the ridiculousness of his situation.

But bring him onto the Sugarbabe?

Good gawd.

Wildcat would kill her.

"If you take me with you, I will help you on your ship. I have been programmed on many aspects of machinery. You will not regret it. Please, I must leave here."

"Look, *Slick*, even if I wanted to, I couldn't. I'm sorry. You're the property of the Slide consortium. They wouldn't take kindly to me stealing such an expensive piece."

As soon as the words left her mouth, she knew how they sounded. She flushed.

"Piece of equipment," she amended.

"Oh, for suck's sake, Lucky, take him. How can you leave that face and body behind? It will haunt you forever, girl. He just wants to be free. He's– he's asking you for asylum!"

"Spin, he is an android. This is not some dramatic bid for sanctuary. He is a machine. You are overreacting."

"You don't know that. Besides. . ." He leaned in and whispered so loudly that there was no way the android could not hear him. "Once he's on the ship he can do double duty– if you get my drift. Just think of it, your own private Masterstroke 6000. With no complications."

She hesitated. It sounded almost too good to be true. There were always complications.

Especially when Spin was around! The Floop had a way of making the most outrageous stuff sound perfectly okay.

"I will do what he says and more, mistress." Kerreth looked her over from head to toe. "Gladly."

The android smiled rather suggestively at her.

Chills skittered down her spine.

Something in that smouldering look did her in.

Sensing her confusion, Kerreth slyly added, "I have

already disengaged my link from the main computer. They will not discover I am missing for several nights. By that time, we could be long gone."

Lucky chewed the inside of her cheek, mulling it over. She hated to abandon anyone; especially someone who had specifically *asked* to be set free. She had strong feelings about freedom– a trait she and her brother both shared.

If she left him, she would feel guilty over it forever.

"Won't they wonder what happened to you when you don't show up for periodic maintenance or appointments?"

"They will assume I had to be scrapped. I have seen this happen before. There will be no risk to you." Kerreth closed the deal by softening the expression in his eyes, instantly placing himself in the heart-tugging category of an abandoned pup.

A little cry of sympathy issued from SpinDrift. "I don't know about you, but I am not leaving him!"

Hook. Line. And sinker. Lucky wanted to give in too. Shoot, Wildcat would *kill* her. Her brother still hadn't gotten over SpinDrift. And that was ten years ago!

The android gave her a big grin of pearly whites. "You will be most pleased with this decision, mistress."

"Look, I appreciate your need for new experiences– if I had to do what you do, I'd go nutzoid too. But. You belong to the Slide Corporation. It wouldn't be right to take you with us. I'm sorry."

He stared deeply into her eyes. He spoke beguilingly. "You would leave me to languish here forever?"

Lucky swallowed. Why did she feel for this machine? She was getting dewy-eyed over a blender. She was hopeless.

"Well. . . I . . ."

Sensing that she was weakening, Kerreth honed in on the finish. "I would be invaluable to you on your ship. I can do many things for you. I can learn. You must need help with something on your ship?" His eyes actually became moist. It was a terrific touch.

Lucky's lips parted. "Well. . .

"Flickerin' finishes, Lucky! Let him come with us! I can't take anymore!" SpinDrift sobbed out loud, wiping his eyes with a scraggly feather he plucked out of his side.

And that was how Kerreth vos Volent got aboard the Sugarbabe.

EPISODE FOUR:
PUTTING IT TO THE TEST

The Sugarbabe

He was not going to get his own cabin.

Or any cabin for that matter.

Apparently androids did not warrant accommodations. Even legendary Masterstroke 6000's.

Once Kerreth got on board their ship, it hadn't taken him long to realize that the *Sugarbabe* was a ragtag clunker of a scow glued together with various piles of scrap parts from the asterheap junkyards.

He hoped it was space-worthy.

They had a long trip ahead of them and there were few way stations along the journey. None of them safe.

Travellers in this sector of the galaxy were known for passing stranded ships and leaving those inside to rely on the kindness of the next stranger to come by.

Most times, that next stranger would rob the marooned vessel.

It was premature for him to worry about the ship's operations; he had to scout out the interior first. Not having a designated place to sleep could be a problem, but nothing he couldn't work around.

It wasn't like he hadn't stowed away on ships before. Sometimes it turned out good. Sometimes... real, real *bad.*

This job, however, was imbuing him with optimism. He was sure he was 'this close' to claiming that sweet slice of miadne. A little creative scheduling... a hidden corner for sleeping... a mid shift sneak into the showers and galley– he'd work it out.

In their haste to depart Slide to examine whatever they had found in the vase, the redheaded woman and the Floop had abandoned him in the cargo bay and dashed up to the bridge.

Temporarily left to his own devices, it hadn't taken long for Kerreth to run into the ship's engineer.

The big, square *Kelvinator* was monitoring the engine's readouts, completely uninterested in the newcomer. He did not even turn from his console to acknowledge Kerreth's presence.

Kelvinators usually greeted strangers by offering them the cold shoulder. It was their way of saying 'how-do!' Unfortunately, no one really understood that.

Kerreth was no exception.

"Thanks for the warm welcome, friend," he muttered under his breath.

"Ur." came the disinterested reply.

Kerreth rolled his eyes and exited the cargo bay.

***

"So, what do you all think it is?"

Lucky bent over SpinDrift's bony shoulder to gaze at the monitor. They had literally fed the chip to Minmei– who had coughed it back up at first, then dutifully swallowed it and displayed it for them on the ship's screens.

"Maybe it's some kind of message. . . ?" SpinDrift cocked his head to the side as he viewed the blurry object.

Minmei continually rotated the item, as if that would help them decipher it.

"I have no idea." Lucky scratched the back of her head.

"Urrrrrrrr." Clugot was obviously on the fence too.

Minmei yawned rather loudly. Apparently it was not easy being a computer with a short attention span.

Exasperated, Lucky threw up her arms. "Doesn't anyone have a clue as to what it is?"

She felt something rigid press into her thigh.

Lucky gritted her teeth. Since the android had come on the bridge a while ago, he had stuck to her like glue. "Stop leaning in so close to me, Slick! We are trying to work. Can't you go to your quarters until I call for you?"

"No mistress."

"Why not?"

"I do not have any quarters."

"Fine– go to my quarters!"

Kerreth shook his head. "I cannot. I must observe what transpires aboard this ship."

"Why?"

"How else am I to help you?"

"We don't need your help."

SpinDrift leaned towards Lucky and spoke in a singsong

voice. "Maybe we do-o-o. It couldn't hurt; we're getting no-o-o-o-where."

True. "Well, move back and quit crowding me, Slick. Geesh!"

"As you say." He moved back half an inch.

Lucky rolled her eyes. *How come machines never get it?! Who the hell programs these excuses for extreme annoyance?*

Minmei gave a dainty hiccup and giggled.

Lucky slapped her forehead with the heel of her hand. *Argh!*

"Whatever is on that chip seems to be locked."

Minmei concurred.

"THIS IS TRUE, I CANNOT GET INSIDE FOR YOU."

Kerreth leaned over Lucky's shoulder and pointed at the rotating, fuzzy image of the chip. "Can you clean this image up?"

"Well, I–"

"Not you; I was speaking to your ship. You do have an integrated systems op on this– " He looked around the deck with distaste. "– ship?"

"Of course we do!" Lucky bristled. The Sugarbabe might not look like much but she could outrun most corporate ships in a pinch. Wildcat had wisely put their money where he thought it counted: getaway power. All things considered, Mama Bros had patched together a pretty decent (if pitchy) system.

"Poor folk make *do*, you know?" Lucky whispered to Spin. "Seems the Masterstroke 6000s are kind of a snobby bunch."

"From what I've heard they have every right to be." Spin whispered back.

Minmei addressed Kerreth sweetly.

"YOU WISH ME TO CLEAR THE IMAGE?"

"Can you sharpen it up for me?" he purred back.

Minmei was smitten.

"OH, YES! *TEE-HEE-HEE.*"

Lucky's mouth opened and her tongue dropped out. Thereby showcasing her extreme nausea.

Kerreth almost lost it by coughing. *Until it hit him that she was utterly adorable.* A line furrowed his smooth brow. *Why didn't he notice that before?*

Maybe he did. . . but ignored it for the sake of the job at hand.

Could she be trouble?

He sneaked a peak at her. Luscious full lips. Sweet upturned nose. Expressive, round green eyes . An asteroid's worth of curly red hair. And a real cheeky personality.

Oh, yeah, she could be serious trouble.

"Do you see anything?" Lucky scrutinized the image with him.

He saw something; only not on the screen. Yeah, he was *very* attracted to her.

"I know I do." He viewed her from under his dark lashes. "Do you?" he murmured right next to her ear.

The Masterstroke's hot breath skittered along Luckys lobe.

She jumped. Simulated breathing? *They even added warmth for realism*! Amazing. And a little scary. "Um. . . could you not do that?"

"Do what?" His warm lips almost touched her ear.

Lucky opened her mouth to let him have it but SpinDrift forestalled her. "For lick's sake, Lucky, he *is* a pleasure droid. You can't expect him to ignore his programming entirely."

"Why not?"

"I *am* programmed to seduce." Kerreth shrugged his shoulders.

"Well, *un*program yourself."

Spin examined one of his claws. "I doubt he can."

"I doubt I can." Kerreth agreed.

Lucky clenched her fists. "I swear, I will put you both off this ship if–"

"What are those markings on the side of the chip?"

"–you continue. . . where?" Lucky studied the screen.

"Here." Kerreth pointed to an area of the image that looked fuzzier than the rest.

"I don't see anything. Do you, SpinDrift?"

"Just some scratches on the casing."

"Those aren't scratches. Minmei. . . ?" Kerreth looked to the console for both an acknowledgement of the proper address, as well as a direct response."

"YE-E-E-S-S-S?"

Hesitant. Shy. Yet game for fun. *You could almost see the pigtails, pleated miniskirt, and sailor blouse.*

Lucky made a face at the computer.

"Could you enlarge this section of the picture for us?"

"FOR YOU, I WOULD DO IT."

Minmei's breathy tone made it clear that she would like to do much more for the android than simply enlarge an image.

The picture in front of them immediately swelled to ten times its normal size, filling the screen to the edge of the border. It spilled over to the screen on the far wall.

The implied message was not subtly done; the resulting image was impossibly *huge.*

"She never responds to me like that," Lucky groused to Spin.

"She does to Sensei Arrows, though."

Lucky grimaced. When it came to user interface, Minmei was a total gender whore.

"Hmmm . . ." Kerreth stroked his jaw. "What do you make of that, Red?"

"Wishful thinking on Minmei's part?"

Kerreth's lips twitched. "Ah, I meant the image."

"Oh. Um. . . looks like even bigger scratches."

"Look closer; they're arrows."

SpinDrift gasped. "He's right! They are arrows! What does it mean?"

"I was hoping you could tell me." Kerreth stared at Lucky, expecting some kind of revelation.

"I have no idea!"

He quirked his brow. "Perhaps, Ms. *Arrows*, there *is* a connection between you and the chip that was left in a vase in the room belonging to the being who apparently boarded the last ship out of Volauvent after the Heart of the Merchandiser went missing?"

SpinDrift almost swooned. "Oh, oh, he sounds just like Poirot!"

Lucky ignored the Floop's buddying-up. Slick didn't seem

at all like the Hercule type to her. Not one bit. She responded to him in kind. "That is ridiculous, Mr. *Slowhand.*"

Okay, that sounded real stupid.

"In case you've forgotten, Slick, we are *looking* for that jewel. Why would there be a connection?"

"I'm not sure, but there appears to be one."

SpinDrift dropped his head and solemnly quoted the Belgium bloodhound. "Mon ami, what will you? You fix upon me a look of dog-like devotion and demand of me a pronouncement a la Sherlock Holmes!"

Lucky thought the android's programming had disconnected for a second because he just stood there and seemed to go *clunk.*

"What is he talking about?" Kerreth jerked his thumb in the Floop's direction.

"The same thing we're all talking about– the jewel. There's something I don't get, though. . ."

"Take a number."

"How did you know that only one ship had left Volauvent after the theft occurred?"

Kerreth blinked and did what *he* was famous for. Thought fast. "I scanned your ship's last transmissions from the cargo bay."

That was suspicious. "Why would you do that?"

"I wanted to be sure that the Slide Consortium was not alerted to my absence. I used your ship's sensors instead of my own to ensure that they could not track me via the transmission."

"Oh."

"Yes."

"If only we had something else to go on." Lucky chewed her lip.

Kerreth spoke in a sexy drawl to the computer. "Minmei, is there anything else you can tell me about the chip?"

"THERE IS A FIBER ATTACHED TO THE CHIP, SLOWHAND-SAN. IS IT OF ANY SIGNIFICANCE?"

Slowhand-san. Lucky was this close to pulling Minmei's plug out. The recently grovelling computer never tried this hard for her and Spin.

"I don't know, Minmei. Why don't you tell me?" Kerreth whispered.

He could coax a hermit into a mosh pit. Lucky sighed then felt immediately better when she realized what all that expert programming could do for the Sugarbabe.

No matter.

Wildcat was still going to kill her.

"THIS FIBER IS COMPRISED OF SKEKZIN; IT IS USED IN MANY MATERIALS FOR ITS DURABILITY. SKEKZIN IS COOL IN WARM CLIMES AND WARM IN COOL CLIMES. IT BLENDS–"

"Any unusual traits?" Kerreth interrupted her.

"MANY. *TEE-HEE-HEE.*"

Lucky nodded. *There* was their Minmei. Back again and ditsy as ever. She reckoned pleasure droids were programmed to lose their patience as a way to increase the illusion that they were like real men.

Slick might be dripping testosterone– but ol' *Slowhand-san* looked like he was about to pop a cork.

"Care to tell me a few?" he gritted out.

Lucky, knowing what was coming, made ready to abridge

the response for him.

"SKEKZIN IS STRUCTURED AS A PHOTOSYNTHETIC, EUKARYOTIC ORGANISM. . ."

"A plant." Lucky helpfully translated.

Kerreth crossed his arms and leaned back against one of the consoles. Clearly, he was prepared to wait it out.

". . . WHOSE FIBER IS UTILIZED IN THE PRODUCTION OF. . . "

"Woven." Lucky supplied.

". . . THESE FIBERS BY WAY OF THE PROCESS OF WEFT AND WARP. . ."

"Fabric."

". . . SKEKZIN IS INDIGENOUS TO DUMFUG 8; GROWING EXCLUSIVELY ON THE SANDY TERRACES OF THE SLOPES OF–"

"Whoah." Kerreth stood. "Are you saying this fiber only grows in this one place and nowhere else?"

"THAT IS WHAT I AM SAYING, SLOWHAND-SAN."

Minmei put on the screen a composite rendering of the fabric based on the fiber sample.

Ug-leeee.

"Is the fabric exported?"

"NO, SLOWHAND-SAN. SKEKZIN IS CONSIDERED A SACRED PLANT ON DUMFUG 8. FABRIC WOVEN FROM THIS PLANT CAN ONLY BE WORN BY A DUMFUG."

"No argument there." Lucky viewed the fabric with distaste.

A huge grin spread across Kerreth's face. He could learn to love that nasty fabric because it just brought that wondrous hunk of miadne that much closer to his hands. "We just got real lucky, Lucky."

"That was the clue we were hoping for?"

Kerreth nodded. "That was our clue."

"Good. You know, you have helped us, Slick. I'm almost glad we brought you onboard."

Kerreth winked at her. "It was sure *Lucky* for me."

Her cheeks colored. He was playing her all right.

"Minmei, send a course for Dumfug 8 to Clugot." Lucky punched the link to the engine room. "Clugot, we're heading to Dumfug 8; we'll need all the speed you can give us. If we got this far on the hunt, others will too. We can't afford to lose that prize."

"Urrr." Clugot out.

Lucky stretched, spreading her arms wide to work the kinks out of her back. "Now we can relax until–"

"MINMEI HAS EMERGENCY! MINMEI HAS EMERGENCY!"

Lucky snapped upright. "*What?* We just started out!"

SpinDrift waddled by. "Oh, it can't be anything too serious; you know our Minmei."

"THE SHIP WILL EXPLODE IN FORTY-FOUR POINT THREE MINUTES. *TEE-HEE-HEE.*"

"WHAT?!"

"*What?*"

"Braaaak!"

Everyone started talking at once. Except for Spin who was running around in circles clucking hysterically.

"What is going on?" Lucky demanded of the console.

"What is the danger?" Kerreth snapped the question more like an order. Even though this wasn't his ship, he damn well knew how to captain one.

"Ur?" Even Clugot wanted some answers. Quick.

"*YOU* ARE THE DANGER, SLOWHAND-SAN."

Kerreth blinked. Once. "What is that supposed to mean, exactly?"

"YOU ARE A MASTERSTROKE 6000, IS THAT NOT CORRECT?'

"Yes," he responded, warily.

"MASTERSTROKE 6000'S ARE THE MOST ADVANCED PLEASURE DROIDS EVER BUILT. YEARS OF RESEARCH WENT INTO THE DESIGN AND IMPLEMENTATION OF A LIFELIKE AI THAT CAN REPLICATE HUMANOID SEXUAL INTERACTIONS TO WITHIN .05846 DEGREE OF ACCURACY."

Kerreth, wise now to Minmei's roundabout explanations, barked out, "Get on with it!"

"YOU ARE VERY EXPENSIVE, SLOWHAND-SAN."

Lucky's brow furrowed. "To use?"

"TO DEVELOPE. BECAUSE OF THIS, YOU WERE BUILT WITH A FAIL-SAFE MECHANISM."

SpinDrift screeched to a halt. "What kind of fail-safe?"

Lucky added, "Will he shut down or something?"

"NOT LIKELY, MISS LUCKY AND MASTER FLOOP. HIS POWER CENTER IS SEATED IN HIS TITANIUM CROTCH."

"Get out of here." Lucky and Spin both looked in the direction of the object of all the fuss.

Kerreth glared back at them.

"IT IS A FACT." Minmei went on. "THERE IS A THERMO-NUCLEAR DEVICE IMPLANTED IN THE REGION OF HIS TESTES."

"Good grief, what next!" Lucky did not expect a response from anyone. Nevertheless, Minmei gave her one.

"THE RESULTANT EXPLOSION WILL ELIMINATE THIS SHIP. . . EVERYONE ON IT. . . SEVERAL NEARBY SATELLITES. . . AND POSSIBLY. . . CLUTCH CHOMPS' FLY-THRU SHIP WASH AND

QUICKIE MART."

SpinDrift wailed. "Oh no, not Clutch Chomps! Where will I play my numerics?! My scratch cards?" He turned on Kerreth and pointed directly at his groin. "We have to get rid of it!"

"Don't even think it, Floop boy." Kerreth looked ready and willing to defend the 'territory'.

"Spin's been playing *Gotta Win* for a long time." Lucky explained. "He's hasn't won yet."

"Hmf!" SpinDrift sniffed. "You don't win unless you *play* and I won't be able to play if he blows up Clutch Chomps. "

"Not to mention half this sector," Lucky grumbled. "Why would they put something like that in him? It's dangerous. A lot of people could get killed– not to mention us."

"THEY HAVE FOUND IT TO BE AN EFFECTIVE MEASURE AGAINST ANYONE STEALING OR TRANSPORTING A MASTER-STROKE 6000," Minmei explained helpfully.

"But we didn't steal him! He came along of his own accord."

"IT DOES NOT MATTER, MISS LUCKY. ONCE WE LEAVE ORBIT AND REACH THE CRITICAL RADIUS FROM SLIDE– WHICH I HAVE CALCULATED TO BE IN FORTY-TWO POINT FIVE MINUTES– HE WILL GO *BADDA-BOOM*. CORRECTION: MAKE THAT BIG BADDA-BOOM."

"Are you absolutely sure that Slick has this implant, Minmei?"

"I AM NOT EQUIPPED WITH THOSE KIND OF SPECIALIZED SCANNING SENSORS; HOWEVER, ALL MASTERSTROKE 6000

UNITS ARE BUILT WITH THIS FAILSAFE. HE IS SET TO BLOW, MISS LUCKY."

"The hell he will! Reverse course immediately, Minmei! We'll just put him back where we got him." She turned to Kerreth. "Sorry, Slick; it's *not* working out."

It was working out just fine as far as he was concerned.

She wasn't getting rid of him that easy.

He had a stake in a certain miadne fantasy; he wasn't going to let them get it without him.

Kerreth straightened up to his full height, towering over her. "It's not that clean, Red. For one, Slide has some nasty corporate partners. Ever hear of Crisyn?"

Lucky paled. Crisyn was the big daddy of crime syndicates; they had deep, malevolent roots and were brazen enough to state exactly the kind of business they engaged in right in their name.

That alone said plenty.

Wildcat had crossed them on a number of occasions. The only reason her brother was still alive to tell the tales was that Crisyn needed his skills from time to time.

Still, they were a scary bunch.

"I can see by your reaction that you get my point. If you think they'll let you just drop me off and walk away, you're wrong. They'll detain you indefinitely by impounding your only way out. They'll take your ship. There's no telling what could happen to you all. Do you want to end up working at the Playhouse like I did, Red? I imagine it would be different for a humanbeing. . . unbearable, perhaps. Am I not right?"

Lucky swallowed. What a fine mess this pleasure droid

had gotten them into! "Don't be ridiculous! I'll explain to the Boss of Slide exactly what happened."

"CHANCES OF BEING BELIEVED ARE 1,867,899,644,001 TO 1."

Kerreth looked pleased at that result. "Thank you, Minmei."

"Well, we can't let him stay! He'll blow up the ship!"

"IN FORTY ONE POINT NINE MINUTES."

SpinDrift crawled on top of one of the consoles. The Floop was on a mission.

Lucky's mouth pursed. "Don't you even think of hanging from that ceiling girder to have a nutty, Spin! I'm warning you!"

Miffed, SpinDrift peevishly climbed down.

"The last time he did that," Lucky confided to Kerreth, "he *quackle-plucked* half his coat off."

"Quackle-plucked?"

"Floop disorder. Carryin' on, cluckin' at the top of his lungs, yankin' out feathers– which clogged up three of Minmei's vents, I might add. What a disaster! Minmei overheated and we had to go to dock for a complete reboot. It was not a happy time, I can tell you."

An image of her brother's icy blue eyes shooting daggers at SpinDrift flashed across her mind.

She gulped.

Wildcat was sure to be angrier over this stunt– if they lived long enough for him to find out.

"I think I'm going to be sick." Lucky clutched her stomach.

Kerreth decided he was in a room full of *quackle-plucker*

jobs.

Minmei interrupted his analysis with the worst assessment he had ever heard out of the 'mouth' of a computer.

"SLOWHAND-SAN, THE MASTERSTROKE 6000 HAS A TWO TIER AI; PRIMAL AND INTELLECTUAL. THE COLLECTIVE AI IS DESIGNED SO THAT ITS INTERNAL PROGRAMMING CORRUPTS AS IT APPROACHES CRITICAL RADIUS FROM ITS ASSIGNED SOURCE."

"I know; big badda-boom."

"AFFIRMATIVE, BUT THE FAIL-SAFE APPEARS TO ONLY BE WIRED INTO YOUR INTELLECTUAL AI."

Lucky perked up. "What is the significance of that?"

None, as far as Kerreth was concerned. His gonads were not going to detonate.

Stupidest thing he ever heard.

Still, he listened dutifully all the same. He had to find out if his assessment was coming out on the positive side.

"THERE IS NO FAIL-SAFE IN SLOWHAND-SAN'S PRIMAL AI. IF THIS PRIMAL AI IS ACTIVATED, IT SHOULD OVERRIDE THE INTELLECTUAL AI AND ALL OF ITS DIRECTIVES INCLUDING THE FAIL-SAFE."

"Sounds logical." Lucky tapped her chin. "That doesn't sound too difficult, either."

"IT IS NOT SIMPLE. HIS PRIMAL MUST BE *FULLY* ENGAGED AT THE PRECISE TIME THAT SLOWHAND-SAN HITS CRITICAL RADIUS FROM SLIDE. IF THIS CAN BE ACCOMPLISHED, THEN HIS FAIL-SAFE WOULD DISENGAGE."

"And just how does his primal AI become engaged?"

"SINCE HE IS A PLEASURE DROID, INTENSE SEXUAL ACT-

IVITY WOULD OCCUPY HIS PRIMAL SIDE."

"Oh, hell no." Lucky groaned.

A slow grin revealed Kerreth's white teeth. He chuckled an annoying sequence: *Heh*. Pause. *Heh*. Pause. *Heh heh heh*.

"BE WARNED: A TOTAL SEXUAL IMMERSION MUST BE ACHIEVED AT THE EXACT TIME THE FAIL-SAFE IS PRE-PROGRAMMED TO DETONATE. AT THAT POINT, HIS PRIMAL AI MUST HAVE COMPLETELY TAKEN OVER HIS DIRECTIVES.

Kerreth wondered if he should be insulted. "Minmei, are you saying I can't have sex and think at the same time?"

Lucky guffawed. "Geesh, he *is* just like a real man, isn't he?"

Spin chortled with glee.

"SLOWHAND-SAN, YOU MUST BE COMPLETELY INVOLVED IN WHAT YOU ARE PHYSICALLY DOING AND FEELING TO THE POINT THAT YOU CAN THINK OF NOTHING BUT WHAT YOU ARE EXPERIENCING."

"I get it."

"You can *feel*?" Lucky was surprised.

"So I'm told." He smiled mysteriously.

"MASTERSTROKE 6000'S WERE DESIGNED TO EXPERIENCE AN EQUIVALENT SENSATION TO TOUCH. THEIR CREATORS THOUGHT IT WOULD MAKE THEM MORE RESPONSIVE."

Pause.

"TEE-HEE-HEE."

"No doubt it does." Lucky looked him over and wondered. He feels, he thinks. . . he slices, he dices. Is he self-aware? *He did ask me for asylum. . .*

Spin clasped his claws to his chest. "Looks like you two

have to get lively together or else this ship and everyone in it is history." He sighed. "What do you say to that, Lucky?"

"I say we're all gonna die."

SpinDrift was aghast. "You can't mean that!"

She grimaced. "I am not the one for the job."

SpinDrift's beak fell open. "You're the *only* one for this job."

"I'll second that." Kerreth was really enjoying this. In fact, since he had stumbled onto these two, he had had to fight to keep himself from laughing himself sick.

He hadn't had so much fun in a long time. And he liked it.

"YOU NOW HAVE FORTY POINT ZERO MINUTES UNTIL COMPLETE ANNIHILATION."

Kerreth looked askance at the girl. If anyone could engage him, she could. Those sweet pink lips were making him primal all right. Perfect for the task at hand.

If he was forced to attach credibility to the wild plan.

That mixed-up excuse for a computer system had pulled that fail-safe dross out of its corrupted files.

Thermo-nuclear balls.

Uh-huh.

And those two brain splinters believed it.

He wondered just how far Red would go with the crazy scheme. The trouble was that he was sparked by her. Every time she came near him, his heart beat faster. There was a crackle of electricity between them; he could *feel* it.

Men like him spent their lives going after the uncommon. They coveted it. Risked their lives to seek it out. And if they found it, they treasured it for the rest of their lives.

Lucky Red Arrows was the most 'uncommonest' woman Kerreth had ever met.

Although he was somewhat loathe to admit it, he was charmed.

What had started out as a single retrieval mission was quickly turning into a multilevel treasure hunt. The prize was the miadne jewel– and, possibly, the unconventional gift of a passionate, redheaded woman who knew how to laugh and was more than a scrap of eccentric.

He definitely wanted a taste of both.

"So, Red, where should we go to be alone to save the universe as we know it?" he smoothly inquired.

"THE TIME TO EXTINCTION IS NOW–"

"We get it, Minmei!" Lucky exploded on a resigned sigh. "My cabin, robo boy. *Right now."*

"Looks like I'm gettin' Lucky," Kerreth quipped. "Heh. Heh. Heh."

"Shut up." She sneered at him. There was no way for her to get out of sleeping with him and still live. . . but that didn't mean he had to go all male contender on her either. She stuck a finger in his face. "Just remember this does not come with bragging rights."

"No, Mistress Arrows." His lips twitched.

"If this works and we make it through this, you are not to tell a living soul."

"Yes, Mistress Arrows." He solemnly vowed.

Lucky scrutinized his face for a sign of sincerity, but found what suspiciously looked like amusement. *Why did the developers have to give him a sense of humor?* Did he really need it to do what he did?

On second thought, he probably did.

"Okay, c'mon; let's get this over with."

"My 'fate' will be in your hands, Red." A dimple curved into his handsome cheek. *"Again."*

"Don't even start."

As they left the bridge, SpinDrift's solemn commentary followed Lucky into the elevator. "It is a far, far better thing she does, than she has ever done before!"

Lucky threw her own parting invocation to the Floop as the doors closed. An eloquent, expressive declamation of gesture from her native world.

She extended a middle finger in friendship.

The shocked Floop let out an involuntary exclamation.

"Bra-a-a-a-k!"

EPISODE FIVE:
MEN AT WORK

Onboard the Zoltarian vessel, Bobone

"They say that all the humanoid races are connected in some way."

The pirate ran the tip of her sharp fingernail down the centerline of Wildcat's bare chest. "Do you believe that's true?"

He tossed his mane of hair back. "What does it matter what I believe?"

"You fascinate me. It has been a long time since anyone has done that."

Is that what Zoltarians called it? He smiled to himself. Well, he didn't want to *fascinate* her too much– he needed to get off this ship!

"What is your name, Captain?" he drawled.

"I am known as Kokol: she who has a swift hand."

She stretched against the bed covers. They were remarkably silky for this kind of a ship.

Apparently some Zoltarian pirates did not like to rough it while they were pillaging.

"Did you say your name is Cold Call?" A line furrowed his brow.

She gave him a look "I doubt it."

"Ah."

She had a sense of humor– which was unusual for a Zoltarian.

Too bad he couldn't trust it. Odd things had been done throughout history with a sense of humor.

He ran his fingers gently through her magenta hair, letting the strands tug softly. She liked it. Kokol closed her eyes and arched her back slightly; almost purring.

He watched her reaction with heavy lids.

Even though he was warming up to her, when push came to shove, she was going to sell him down the proverbial river. It wouldn't be personal. It would be plain ol' economics.

It's what pirates did.

Wildcat rested against the back of the bed and stared up at the ceiling. He was worried about Lucky.

His present predicament made him realize that he should see to her future.

Just in case.

He needed more security measures in place. This latest diversion on Cretion had cost him more than he would ever admit.

"Jack Hammer, you are far away."

Wildcat turned his head and looked at her.

"There is something about you. . . " Kokol sniffed his

face.

Wildcat grinned. Her action was rather cute. "Learn anything I should know about?"

"You are a very physical man. . ." Kokol licked her lips. "I like that."

"You found that out just from one sniff, hmm?"

"There is a lot a Zoltarian can tell from a simple sniff. You would be surprised."

"No doubt I would." He caught the tip of her nose between his teeth.

She yelped and laughed at the same time. He grabbed her in his arms and rolled across the bed with her while she was still laughing.

He ended up on top. She grinned up at him.

"Tell me, you asked to be put off at our next docking. . . but is there not somewhere I can take you? This ship is at my disposal. If I am *put* in the right mood, I can take you anywhere you wish to go."

Wildcat was not fooled by the offer.

She had heard about the stolen miadne. She was wondering if he was on the hunt for it– he could see it on her face.

In fact, that might have been the reason she and her co-pirates were on Cretion in the first place; they were looking for information, and criminals almost always had it.

All decent pirates had good contacts in the prisons.

He watched her carefully.

Could he safely use her offer to get back to his ship?

He knew he couldn't trust her, but he still might be able to use her.

In a good way.

Without anyone getting hurt.

Or sold off for parts.

Kokol laughed. "Such a brooder! You think too much. Why so worried? Come, you can tell me– do you have a special place to go?"

"We all have special places to go sooner or later."

Kokol played with a strand of his hair. It was incredibly silky. "Caution is good; but don't squander an opportunity."

He moved off of her onto his side.

Resting his head in his palm, he said, "I'd rather squander an opportunity than be squandered by one, madam."

"I like that."

"What do you like?" He ran his fingertip over her full lips.

"The way your voice changed just then. . ."

He stilled. "In what way?"

"Your tone became. . . I'm not sure. . . more formal, I suppose. Different. I don't know how to describe it."

"I was just teasing you in my way," he responded gently. "That's all."

"What is your real name?"

His lips curved up at the corners. "Didn't fool you with that one, hmmm?"

"I have an excellent translator– the best that I could steal." She gave him a gamine grin. "I even understood the humor, Jack Hammer."

"Serves me right." He tweaked her chin. "It's Wildcat."

"As in Arrows? You're that famous tracker!" Her eyes took on an avaricious gleam.

Now he knew positively that she knew about that damn gem.

"Guilty as charged, ma'am."

"My respects. Zoltarians admire the job you performed on Hectorari. That was quite a coup for you."

Great. Now he was admired by Zoltarian pirates. That couldn't be good.

"Like you, we Zoltarians are no friend to the Corporations."

"Not all of them are bad."

"Just most, yes?" She playfully slapped his chest.

"Next you'll be having me sign up to go a-viking with you." His ice blue eyes glinted. He didn't have the heart to tell her he could do her work quite well.

Job security was important to pirate captains.

She snickered and ran the tips of her sharp nails over his muscular arms. "Nice. Are you a fighting man?"

"I'm a lover, madam, not a fighter."

She looked at him askance. The man was a potent package of brains, brawn, and talent. Despite what he said, he was built like a warrior. He would make a glorious Zoltarian! "Of course you are."

"Didn't I prove it yet?" He reached for her.

"You must have been in those orzon mines a long time."

"Too long. Come here, my piratess." He brought her lips down to his.

Kokol had already experienced one of his kisses. It had been strangely devastating. . .

Just like his lovemaking.

Nevertheless, he intrigued her.

If she wasn't careful, she might succumb to his charms. That was something she could not afford to do.

She placed her palm between them to forestall him. "Have you never had a true affection for anyone?" she asked curiously.

The sky blue eyes instantly clouded over.

"Don't go soft on me, Captain." He intoned the chilly warning in a voice that clearly warned her to back off.

It was an invitation to one such as she.

Kokol roared with laughter. *"Me?* I wouldn't dream of it. One has to have a heart to go soft." She grabbed his hand and placed it over her left breast. "As you can see, Arrows, I have none."

Wildcat arched a brow. "Really." He moved their hands to the other side, just under her right breast. "What's this?"

She wagged her finger at him. "Well, I don't have a heart where it counts to an Earthman."

Wildcat thought that was probably true.

Zoltarians were known for being incredibly mercenary. "You don't have to convert me; I'm already a believer in your wickedness." He brought their joined hands to his lips and kissed hers.

She grinned and pushed him over onto the cushions. "So many similarities. . . and yet, so many differences."

"Vive la difference."

"Ah, another of your Earth dialects. Interesting how many you know."

He shrugged, noncommittal on that point.[4]

Kokol ran her palm along the leather waistband of Wildcat's pants. He had recently donned them along with his moccasin boots because he needed to explore her ship. He was hoping he had tired her out, but she didn't seem very sleepy. In fact, she was getting frisky again.

Wildcat believed in always having a good exit strategy.

Although he was a man who loved women as often and as well as he could– he did not like to be told he *had* to.

He liked Kokol and he was grateful that the Zoltarian captain had taken him onboard her ship. He had almost gotten over that thing they do with their teeth. Almost.

But he could not forget that first and foremost this woman was a pirate. If a more lucrative deal came her way, she would sell him out at the first opportunity.

She would owe it to her crew, if nothing else.

It was time to renegotiate.

He clasped Kokol's wrist to stop her downward spiralling motion. "Kokol, what if instead of continuing with our original bargain. . . I share with you the co-ordinates of a Class One Crisyn asset ship? It would be a fair exchange for whatever you went to Cretion for. As you

---

[4] One of the major corporations had perfected language issues between the various intelligent civilizations in the local group of galaxies long before Earth had been a twinkle in the sun's eye. It was reckoned it was a good thing if it made it easier to engage in business. Unfortunately, it also had a tendency to blend slang with regional cooking. Guacamole for instance, became guacacois– which eventually turned back to 'that bland green stuff'.

English was the dominant language on Earth and soon emerged as one of the most widely used in space. Sadly, the other Earth languages were quickly relegated to ancient tongues as they fell by the wayside. Cervelles de veau, or veal's brain, became difficult if not impossible to order. Which was not necessarily a bad thing for those not French.

Wildcat had always been particularly fond of the French and Latin languages, to name a few, and was known to frequently pepper his speech with such; thus labelling himself an eccentric.

know, Crisyn asset ships run heavy."

"But why would I want to do that?" She ran her open mouth over his jaw line. The points of her teeth scraped lightly along the skin. The action brought with it a vision of that *other* thing they did with their teeth. He tried not to shudder.

"Think of the treasure, Kokol. I'm talking Class One here."

Kokol extended one of her fingernails, instantly turning it into a weapon. "What if you honor our original bargain, Earthman? Then I will think of letting you off at the next stop. . . or wherever you want to go."

"C'mon now, sugar, there's plenty of treasure to go around for all. No need to get overly greedy."

"Why do you wish to enter into this new bargain? Are you not entranced by me?" She sat up on her elbows and arched her back in a comically sexy pose.

Yeah, he kinda was.

In a friendly way.

Definitely not a romantic way.

Despite being locked up for six months– and certainly overdue for some entrancement– all he could think of was getting back to the Sugarbabe.

He needed to find out if his crew was all right.

Of course, there was no way he was going to tell her that. "I, ah, I am very attracted to you." He bent his head to nibble on the side of her breast. The tips of his hair brushed over the pointed pink nipples.

Pointed nails. Pointed teeth. Pointed nipples. She was the pointiest woman he had ever met.

A man could do worse, he supposed, grinning against her plump breast. He bit her sharply. Just the perfect amount of sting.

She shivered. "You are something delectable, are you not?"

Wildcat shrugged but his azure irises glittered down at her between the black crescents of spiky lashes.

"I could sense that back in the bar, you know. You are, shall we say, a special *treat*."

He continued to watch her through the veil of lashes. "I might be too much of a treat for you."

She threw back her head and laughed. "I will take my chances, tracker."

"Very well. Don't say I didn't warn you."

"Understood."

"Do you mind if I clean up? Nothing like a good scrubbing to make it all new again. No tellin' how good that'll make you feel."

Kokol snickered. "Of course not. Just don't remove too much of your scent. I like it."

"Wouldn't think of it, Captain," he murmured dryly. He rolled off the Zoltarian bed and stood over her. "Where is the whatever you call a shower on board this ship?"

"There is a cleansing station down the corridor. It is located in the first entrance to your left."

"My thanks." He swept her a bow.

She stopped him at the door to her cabin. "Arrows."

"Mmm?"

"I should warn you that you might find the experience less than pleasant. I have heard from several other captives that our chemical cleansing spray was rather harsh to them."

Her use of the word captive did not go unnoticed by him. Wildcat would bet she had no intention of letting him off at the next stop or any other stop. She probably was looking to use him and then sell his body for spare parts.

"Thank you, Captain. I will give your warning the consideration it deserves."

"After you return, you will engage with me. Then you will tell me where this Crisyn asset ship is."

"Changing the terms of the proposal, are we? If I recall, I said I'd tell you where the Crisyn ship is *after* you release me."

"Make me beg first." She whispered teasingly.

He inclined his head in a mock salute before he left.

The lady wasn't all bad.

She was just drawn that way.

* * *

He left the room and strolled down the main corridor from her cabin.

That was when it occurred to him that Zoltarians had to be the worst housekeepers in the galaxy. The corridor was filled with junk. Old parts. Clothing. Stuff that looked like trash.

Trash that looked like stuff. . .

You name it, it was tossed along the hallway.

The entire ship was a mobile flea market. Even Mama Bros Not Quite Used Emporium was neater than this– and that was saying something since Mama Bros *was* a junkyard.

Well, a junkyard/tavern/cafe to be exact.

On the way to the cleansing station– and he could hardly wait to see that setup– he passed by several of the crew.

The Dawg Pound all took turns to curl a lip at him.

Ah, to be made welcome.

"Have a nice day!" He blithely waved at a passing scalawag.

The Zoltarian growled and kept walking.

Well, at least they were leaving him alone.

As their captain's new exerciser, he was probably safe for the time being. From the crews response Wildcat gathered that 'playing with supper' was a regularly scheduled event for this captain. The rest of the crew was patiently waiting for him to be converted into an actual treat.

Apparently they had enough fear of her to let him be. *She must be the alpha bitch.*

Which was good or bad, depending.

Note to self: do not underestimate Kokol.

As he moved down the hallway, a dark shadow dogged his steps.

He stopped in front of the first door on the left.

Wildcat entered the room designated as the cleansing chamber. Like everything else on this ship, it looked like it needed cleansing.

He approached the sanitizer on the wall. "Let's see. . . No instructions but I'm betting this lever here–"

An image of him bent over and gagging as the sanitizer turned on instantly flashed into his head. He saw himself too dizzy to stand. This so-called chemical shower would react on him like a drug.

"Thanks for the warning," Wildcat murmured.

The shadow moved along the wall.

Wildcat crossed his arms over his chest. "What took you so long to get to me on Cretion?"

The shadow wafted directly in front of him.

"I expected you a lot sooner, Cloud."

A dark film wavered into a partial shape. A non-apologetic shape.

"You left me in that hellhole for six months." Wildcat tapped his moccasin against the steel floor.

A slow grin appeared within the nebulous figure. White teeth glinted with a flash, then disappeared in smoke.

It reminded Wildcat of a dangerous Cheshire cat.

"Not sure what you find enjoyable about the situation. It was not a pretty vacation. So where were you?"

A vision of the four beautiful Mysitkian mountains rose in front of Wildcat. He was not sure what *that* meant– except that the Auran had been detained. With mountains? Sometimes Cloud's images were to be poetically interpreted.

The grin reappeared; wider this time.

"Alright; so you know I don't know what that means. Dammit, Cloud, quit jerking me around."

Cloud partially materialized in front of him.

Wildcat could see right through him. He was an amorphous being from a race of twilight assassins. Highly skilled in stealth and killing. Aurans– when they could be counted on to work for hire– were the best known weapons in the universe. *Living weapons.*

Wildcat was one of the few who could readily converse with a member of their species. Some said it was a natural talent; but no one knew why some could and most couldn't.

Wildcat did not know why he was able to 'talk' with Cloud either; he just knew he could. Aurans communicated telepathically with pictures. Both in your head and out. He wondered if they understood spatial relationships differently.

Most could not engage with beings outside their own species.[5]

As far as the Aurans were concerned, no one knew too much about them save that they were excellent killers.

Thus, their feared reputation.[6]

For a reason Wildcat had never quite figured out, Cloud had decided he was going to work for *him;* even though he never actually hired him or went looking for him. He was not sure what he had done to get his very own Auran; but he suspected he would one day find out.

Cloud had just appeared one day and had stuck with him ever since. Over time, the two had become fast friends.

If one could become friends with an assassin.

Still, Wildcat trusted Cloud with his life and would risk

---

[5] The few Aurans who were able to communicate were sought after by all the big Corporations. Inhouse hitmen that were fast, lethal, untraceable, and had a zero percent failure rate were on the fast track for the best deferred investment plans. Of course, The Yooge Syndicate– which controlled a vast number of the lesser corporations– had to approve the fatwah first. And they all had very specific guidelines of company policy relegated to hits. Assassinations weren't sanctioned just because someone wanted to take out a frisky competitor. No sirree. That policy would quickly lead to anarchy. There were *memos.* And they had best be followed.

[6] Many corporations tried desperately to compete for an Auran when one made itself known. Aurans were very particular who they worked for and they did not seem to pick their jobs for the miadne alone.

his own to save the Auran.

He was sure Cloud knew that.

Sometimes he wondered if the Auran had somehow 'adopted' him.

Crazy notion, but there was no tellin'.

Most did not know Wildcat travelled with his own personal assassin and he intended to keep it that way.

For both their sakes.

Every corporate skunk would be on Wildcat's tail if they thought they could reach an Auran through him.

"We have to get back to the *Babe* as soon as possible."

Cloud agreed.

"I don't think our hosts are completely honorable, buddy."

. . . an image of Kokol selling the Sugarbabe to the black-market Nugnug formed in his head. . .

"Exactly. Any ideas?"

It was unusual for someone to receive Auran images, but it was even more unusual for an Auran to interpret spoken language. As far as Wildcat knew, Cloud was the only one of his species to have that ability.

"Any thoughts on how to get free of our hosts?"

. . . Wildcat saw himself jumping ship when it docked. . .

He discounted the idea. "Too risky. There's no guarantee I could do it even with your help. We're outnumbered fifty to one. And let's not forget these are Zoltarians; Kokol's sure to take extra precautions if they dock at a terminal."

Cloud seemed annoyed that Wildcat had so little faith in his abilities. An image of a shipload full of dead pirates seared into his brain, re-emphasizing the Auran's initial getaway plan.

"Yeah. I know you can do that. I just don't want you to."

Cloud's form wavered in and out. The slight smile, when visible, was utterly chilling. If the Auran could've talked, he would have said, "It would be my pleasure to do it."

Wildcat pointed a finger at him. "You're scaring me, pal."

Cloud grinned.

"Have you heard from Lucky?"

. . . Cloud leaving the ship right after Wildcat disappeared . . .

"You started looking for me right away? And here I thought you didn't care. So, no word from the Sugarbabe I take it?"

. . . A spaceship twirling wildly through space. . . Spin-Drift running around clucking his head off. . . Clugot staring fixated at a console. . .

Wildcat chuckled. "Yep. No tellin' what they've done. We've gotta get back a.s.a.p."

Cloud was in agreement. Both believed that the longer they were away, the least likely the Sugarbabe and its crew would remain in one piece.

. . . Wildcat wrestling with Kokol on her bed. . .

"Hell, no. I'm not sleeping with her again."

Cloud gave him a stare that contained much amusement–yet still managed to retain an air of lethal 'assassin' about it. It was hard to believe an entity who acted as precisely as the Auran did, could, at times, be so very unpredictable.

Wildcat supposed it was the nature of the Auran. Chilling one moment and. . . well, chilling the next.

"She's going to get suspicious if I don't get back there soon."

Cloud whirled over to the disinfector and slashed at it so quickly that if it wasn't for the sound of the tip slicing off the nozzle, Wildcat wouldn't have known it had been split. Cloud gestured to the nozzle indicating that it was now safe for Wildcat to cleanse himself.

"Thanks." Wildcat stepped under the spigot. A spray of fog instantly enveloped him.

If the device was like others he had used on various refueling stations, it should clean and disinfect both him and his clothes at the same time. He threw the shirt he was carrying in front of the spray as well.

"As long as this gets the stink of those orzon mines off me, I will be as happy as a *slubbug.*"

. . . Wildcat stumbling back to the Captain, tumbling onto the bed with her. . . then falling immediately asleep.

Wildcat stroked his jaw. "Not a bad idea. I'll play dead and then she *might* try to contact the Sugarbabe. . ."

The same scene replayed in his head; only this time the Zoltarian in the seductive pose was replaced with a rapidly changing montage of women from Wildcat's past.

Wildcat threw the Auran a withering look. "Yeah, well. . ."

Cloud grinned at his discomfort. It was obvious that Wildcat did not like his past dalliances *replayed for him* in his head.

Which was why Cloud always goaded him with it

whenever the opportunity arose.[7]

"You know, Cloud, I'd be disappointed if Kokol didn't figure out how to reach the ship; especially since I gave her my real name just so she could put it all together."

. . . Kokol ticking off her long fingernails one by one as she tries to count from one to five s-l-o-w-l-y. . . looses her place. . . keeps starting over, confused. . .

Wildcat snorted. "An assassin and a comedian. Who said the Sugarbabe isn't blessed? Let's hope you're right and she's not the brightest star in the Milky Way. We might be able to get out of this relatively unscathed when all's said and done. I just hope Lucky and that noghead SpinDrift haven't done anything stupid in the meantime."

Cloud sent him a brief movie of Lucky looking up into space as if she was getting a great idea! Followed by a series of scenes of natural Earth disasters like the collapse of the Tacoma Narrows bridge in 1940, the great San Franciscan earthquake of 1906, and the Blizzard of 1978, which stalled six lanes of traffic on Massachusetts highways to a frozen standstill for days.

Wildcat understood the message perfectly.

"*Vis inertiae.*" He grunted. "Resistance to inertia is futile." When it came to Lucky and SpinDrift it was a foregone conclusion that trouble was always brewing.

He wondered how much of his ship would still be left for him to actually save.

---

[7] Aurans took great pleasure in making those they associated with squirm every now and then. It was a side effect of the 'assassin' persona and difficult to shed.

EPISODE SIX:
THE MASTERSTROKE 6000

Back on the Sugarbabe

Kerreth could see the skin of Lucky's midriff under the edge of the black shirt she wore. With every step, the soft material slid against that smooth, creamy expanse. He couldn't seem to take his eyes off of that revealing waistband. . .

Which was why he shouldn't have stepped behind to let her lead the way in the first place.

But what choice did he have? He had no idea where her cabin was located.

Stop looking at that skin, dimwit. Do not even gaze at it. You are heading down a dangerous path, Kerreth vos Volent.

There was no way he could stop himself.

She was so delectable. . . !

His heart begin to beat with a familiar heavy *thud thud thud* as he trailed the corridors behind her. Yeah, she had a galaxy-class backside. High, tight, round. A weighty handful.

Just the way he liked it.

If that wasn't temptation enough– he added in the curvy shape, small waist, and spirited, bouncy breasts. He had noted earlier that her breasts also looked like a nice palmful for him.

Not too big. Not too small, either. Just perfect.

And all that crazy, wild red hair!

She was gorgeous.

Best of all, she had none of the boring affectations of the women he was usually put together with– and it would be fair to say he had been with his share. Beautiful women. Sophisticated women.

So why was *this one* getting to him so much?

He needed to keep his distance from her. The Heart of the Merchandiser had to come first.

But that didn't mean he couldn't lead her on for a bit.

If she (and that ridiculous Floop) wanted to believe that his crotch was explosive– Well, for that she deserved a little teasing.

Leading the way, Lucky walked into a closed door. "*Ow!*"

"Ah, are you trying to make yourself unconscious before our big bang arrives?"

"Don't be stupid." She rubbed her nose. "It was supposed to open automatically. This loony tune ship is nothing but spare, two-bit parts; it never works the way it should!"

Frustrated, she kicked the door. It smoothly flowed open for her. "Argh!"

He suppressed a grin. Lucky stormed inside the cabin.

It was clear she was not too happy about the predicament they found themselves in: a stolen Masterstroke 6000, no jewel, extermination imminent, and Wildcat Arrows suspiciously absent. Where was the tracker anyway? There had been no sign of him onboard.

Kerreth followed her inside and gazed around the room.

There wasn't a spare inch of space.

The metal walls were covered with a draping woven fabric that swooped over the narrow bed in a sort of lop-sided canopy. A small desk was cluttered with oddities. Most of them were souvenirs from various worlds– the kind you pick up on a whim at the way station shops. Additional fabrics were draped over a table and scattered clothes were tossed on top of that.

A holo image drifted back and forth over the wall of a smiling Lucky, a tall man with long black hair, SpinDrift, Clugot. . . and the edge of what looked to be some other kind of being.

Metal storage boxes littered the floor. Navigating the room was like going through a maze. Kerreth thought there might be a chair in the corner but there was no telling. And books! He had never seen so many in one place! Most of them looked like love stories.

He never knew anyone from Earth who collected the old things. Nobody from that planet read anymore. At least not from paper.

He bent down and picked up one that had a colorful image on the cover. Science fiction was printed on the spine.

He carefully opened it.

Inside, on the first page, the words 'House of Sages' were printed. And under that *'Property of Wildcat Arrows.'*

So her brother was a reader. Who would have thought it?

By the well-used look of these books, he had passed his love of the written word on to his sister.

Lucky noticed the old book in his hand. "Do you read?"

"Not books and not fiction."

"Why am I not surprised."

She was referring to him being an android.

The truth was he never had the time to sit and read. Perhaps he had been missing something? The corporate syndicates were not supportive of the pastime so maybe there was something to it? He made a note to himself to look into it.

"You know, Lucky, I am not that much different from you."

"Really. And do you dream of electric sheep?"

His brow furrowed. "I don't follow you." He felt like an android in that moment. For flickerin' sake, he even sounded like one! *You do not compute, Mistress Arrows.*

"Tell me about yourself." Lucky looked at him as if he was insane.

"There is no time for us to go through your small talk subroutines for arousal! We have to get on with this immediately! In case you've forgotten, we're all about to go–"

"Badda-boom. I know." He chewed the inside of his cheek. Maybe he wouldn't tease her after all.

She was started to look a tad green around the edges.

He cleared his throat. "Red, I know this is going to sound bad, but please hear me out–"

She tugged her tee shirt over her head and tossed it onto the floor.

Two of the most magnificent breasts he had ever seen bounced in front of his eyes. They seemed to be waving at him. Beckoning him to come and play.

He swallowed.

This was soooo wrong. He couldn't believe he was in this mess! "Ah, favorite food?" he ventured in a low voice.

Lucky put her hands on her hips– which caused her breasts to bob up and down. He was positive he was not looking in her eyes.

"Whatever is the matter with you, Slick?"

"TIME TO ANNIHILATION IS APPROACHING IN EXACTLY THIRTY-SIX MINUTES."

"Do you hear that?" She pointed in the direction of the ceiling, from whence Minmei's voice came. "Quit the 'get her in the right mood' program and strip!"

When his mouth gaped, she added sternly, *"Now, mister!"*

Kerreth viewed her as one would a fascinating, yet slightly mad object of compelling interest. Had he woken up in an alternate universe where young, beautiful women threw off their tops and demanded to be made love to immediately? *Yes, he had!!*

Hot flickerin' shit.

She was really ready to go through with this!

He thought for a moment.

His tingling parts were a pretty good sign that they were going to be perfectly compatible together. Never something to turn your back on.

Should he go ahead and take the chance with her?

Or. . . should he try to talk her out of it?

He wasn't sure he was ready for this but there were advantages to the situation. He had always excelled at finding advantages. It was what he did.

On the one hand, this could be an opportunity for them to get to know each other rather quickly. On the other hand– when all was said and done and revealed– she would probably kill him.

Or more likely, get her brother to do it.

The fact was, this situation had put him in a bind. He was, for all intents and purposes, trapped on this ship until they reached Dumfug 8. (He had often wondered how many Dumfugs there were and was sure the answer was 'more than you can imagine.')

Furthermore, he had no idea what the crew would *do* to him if he revealed the truth.

It was probably not wise or safe for him to blow his cover.

Above all else, he wanted that jewel.

Or more accurately, he *needed* that jewel.

What he was about to do might not be considered noble– but he was what he was. Besides, he had no intention of hurting the girl.

Just the opposite.

If he had a choice, he would give her a memory that would last past any anger she might incur. Like all good memories, it could do away with any hurt.

Foolish as it sounded, Kerreth was kind of. . . sort of. . .

Oh hell. He was taken with her. Or whatever.

So he deluded himself into thinking he just *might* be able to pour on the vos Volent charm, use the opportunity to get closer to her, then call a halt at the right time by telling her the truth.

They were both treasure hunters. She would understand.

She would even see the humor in the situation.

They would all have a good laugh over it!

At least he prayed that was what would happen. By the fiery glint in those green eyes, he was sure she would shoot him with a *crazer* right where he stood if he told her right now.

He began to slowly unzip his uniform.

Her gaze followed the trail of the *zipcro*[8] down past his chest to a point below his waist.

Kerreth glanced up at her and arched an eyebrow. "Favorite spot?" he drawled.

Color filled her cheekbones, but Lucky did not avert her eyes.

The android's golden skin was revealed to her bit by bit by the unfurling cloth.

Beautiful. Taut. Smooth as butter.

Lucky was poleaxed by the glorious sight. *Say what you want about these Masterstrokes– they sure are purty.*

The *zipcro* fastener stopped at an area that was

[8] A version of this particular item will be familiar to Earthlings as hook and loop tape, or velcro. It is a sad but bracing truth that a newly discovered planet loses many of its heretofore exclusive patents to the larger galactic Corporations that hold prior, first dib claims on similar patents filed millennia ago. No discovery is an island, so to speak. Nature abhors a vacuum and so do tinkers. This is referred to throughout the Corporate realms as the nana nana bobo principle of invention. Some have called it an agenda. Cheer up, Earth friends! You still have macadamia nuts.

enticingly shadowed. A slight sheen of moisture buffed the carmel skin.

Lucky's lips parted slightly. "I've always been fond of Kanetium."

Lost, Kerreth cocked his head to the side. "The megaplex on Skryan 3?"

"Yes, have you been there?" Of course, Lucky knew he couldn't have been there; he was an android who was probably built on or directly transported to Slide.

It was hard to remember that looking at him. He was so incredibly male– so *human-like–* that she could even discern the honeyed, musky scent of him.

Kerreth almost answered yes before he caught himself.

"I have seen holos of it. I am sure I would love it *in the flesh* as much as you seem to." He winked suggestively at her.

She was devouring him with her eyes. If things had been different and they had met under other circumstances, Kerreth was sure he would already have had her flat on her back, screaming out his name. His *real* name.

As for Kanetium, it actually was one of his favorite places. The multiplex was open and active all day and all night. He loved it.

Lucky walked over to him and brushed the top of the jumpsuit off his shoulders. Her cool fingers swept against his skin with a frisson of contact.

Kerreth hid his shiver from her.

He was right; that touch was pure ecstasy.

"Are you agreeing with me as part of your seductive technique, Slick? Is that how you get women relaxed and in the mood for you?"

He gave her a lopsided smile. "I would say it is you who is making me relaxed."

"Then I am seducing you?"

"Seems that way."

"I like that." Emboldened, she grazed her lips across his nipples.

The sensation was acute. Kerreth took a deep breath and tried not to clasp her to him.

It was not easy for him to resist the impulse.

Lucky smiled up at him. "You know this is rather freeing in a way– knowing your not judging me."

"*Judging you?* What do you mean?"

"Like a man. Women are always concerned about that; trust me. Am I too thin? Too fat? Too short? Too tall? We always ask ourselves: what is he thinking?"

How about. . . just right. "Who am I to judge you, Red? For that matter, who is any man to judge you?"

Lucky stopped nibbling on the delectable, satiny skin to stare up at him. "I've always wondered that myself. Were you, by chance, programmed by a woman?"

He laughed out loud. "Not yet. But they say there is always hope."

She laughed along with him. "Sense of humor *and* smart, too."

"I'm the whole package, remember?" His arm snaked around her back. He swooped down and kissed her.

The android's firm lips were like velvet clouds. Softly tempting. He playfully brushed her mouth in a quiet dream; back and forth, back and forth.

Lucky shivered.

Without warning, he suddenly sealed his mouth to hers in a hot, forceful taking. Lucky's toes literally curled.

Her fingers clenched.

Heck, everything clenched.

If steam could have come out of her ears, she was sure it would have. *Who kisses like that?* Nobody, she was sure.

When he broke off to stare down at her, he seemed slightly pensive.

Lucky gazed up at him in awe.

True, she hadn't had a lot to compare him with; but she reasoned it was akin to Clugot's upside down *whazzit* cake. You really didn't need to taste any others to know that it was the winning recipe.

"Wow," she whispered, touching her still tingling lips.

"Wow," he whispered back, dipping his head before he could stop himself.

Kerreth kissed her like a man taken. By what, he was not sure.

Nonetheless, he could not seem to stop.

His entire body came alive with her taste. *He was hungry.* Very hungry. The truth suddenly hit him that he was in trouble.

Since Lucky assumed he was an android, she was not at all shy of taking off her clothes in front of a virtual stranger. She kicked off her boots and shrugged out of her jeans, kicking those into the corner with the discarded shirt.

Kerreth watched the items arc across the room, all the while trying to regain his brain. *It isn't going to happen.*

He really couldn't let this happen. . .

But as soon as he caught sight of her standing in front of him buck naked– he was done for. It had been quite a while since his last intimate encounter with a woman; none-theless, he was positive that abstinence was not the reason his tongue was about to hit the floor.

Figuratively speaking.

She was beautiful. And she seemed totally unaware of it.

Of their own accord, his fingers tangled in her hair and his palms cupped the back of her head. He positioned her at the perfect angle for the imminent press of his mouth.

He lowered his head gradually, savoring the prolonged moment. Lucky's green eyes widened slightly just as his lips touched hers.

Decency hit him with a bitch-slap.

Make love to her under these pretences?

He couldn't do it. Sure, he was rogue; but he wasn't a bastard.

No harm in just one more taste, though. . .

Then he was going to call a halt to this ridiculous charade.

"You feel incredible," his voice sounded husky against her mouth.

"Can you actually feel?" Lucky wasn't sure if the an-droid could experience sensation; but he was sure making her feel breathless!

"What do you think?" He didn't give her a chance to re-ply. Instead, he covered her mouth with his own; hot and seeking. Lucky clutched his arms as his tongue thrust into her mouth.

Lucky had heard that the Masterstrokes were so adept at lovemaking that it was difficult to tell them apart from actual human males. The corporation that held their patent had been able to replicate every feature, nuance, sensation, and response of a humanoid male in the throes of sexual desire.

Only this manufactured 'male' never got tired and granted every desire to his erstwhile partner.

There were stories that the Masterstrokes had secret, encoded abilities that were way beyond many humanoid males. This was not greeted with an 'oh happy day' by a large portion of that male population, who naturally feared being upstaged by a machine[9].

Lucky had heard there was talk on several planets of outlawing them all together. For now they were strictly confined to the pleasure planets.

Kerreth's tongue stroked against Lucky's with slow, languorous sweeps. At the same time he massaged her scalp with his entangled fingers, using the same languorous strokes.

She thought his touch just might be magic.

Exactly the right amount of pressure and slide.

The tingling began in her head and swiftly worked its way to her toes. Lucky leaned into the miraculous touch as Kerreth continued to delve between her lips.

She moaned into his mouth.

How could this feel so bloody good?

There was no question that the Masterstroke was getting

[9] Not a new reaction to an improved model, by any means. Humanoid males have been fearing replacement for eons. Some scientists have speculated that this is because a percentage of them equate satisfaction in sexual acts strictly to physical stamina and prowess.

turned on as well. His hold tightened and a distinctive bulge pressed against her lower stomach.

It seemed rather large. . .

Considering his line of work, he was built packing. Lucky's passion-dulled brain distinctly recalled the heft of the weighty package in her palm.

Good grief! Why hadn't she thought of this before?

She hesitated, pulling slightly away from him.

Kerreth– lost in his own desires and having no idea where her fevered thoughts were taking her– brought her firmly back to his side.

He kept right on kissing her. Fiercely, wildly.

If this was to be his only taste, he was making it count. Simple, small pleasures. He decided he could freely give those.

His large hands slid down the cool, velvety skin of her bare back, massaging in ever widening circles. She was soon limp in his arms.

Lucky noticed that the surface of the android's palms were slightly rough. Not perfectly smooth as she would have thought. As a result, the incredible massage was soothing, yet stimulating at the same time.

Once again she marvelled at how his designer had thought of everything.

His designer. Slick wasn't human!

Lucky wondered how she was going to go through with this. She had never been one who went for 'toys' in the bedroom.

Well, survival often changed one's perspective on the deal. Case in point: here she was canoodling with one *elaborate* sex toy.

Go figure the weirdness of life.

"THE TIME TO DESTRUCTION IS NOW THIRTY-FOUR POINT NINE MINUTES."

Both of Lucky and Kerreth broke off from one another to yell at Minmei. *"Shut up!"*

Kerreth recaptured her mouth, taking the opportunity to suckle on her slightly pouty lower lip. He groaned at her lush taste.

"*Red,*" his breath was hot and ragged. "Red. . . you are so sweet. I never would have imagined–"

The rest of his words were lost because Lucky had caught his fire; she began kissing him senseless.

They were two strangers thrown together by sheer chance discovering they liked each other just fine. Kerreth was crazy about her 'feel'. Lucky was going crazy that she was going crazy over the touch of an android!

What could come of it?

Kerreth's palms skimmed down her lower back to slide over her buttocks. If nothing else, he was getting his handful this one time!

He unabashedly clutched the rounded globes in each hand and kneaded himself into an extreme state of arousal. Not thinking, he pressed himself into her. And throbbed.

He could feel the blood coursing through his groin with a heavy beat. *Thud thud thud.* It matched the beat of his heart.

Lucky stopped stroking Kerreth's chest to slip her fingers below his waist, beneath the zipcro edge. They tangled in the musky curls she discovered. Her knuckles skimmed against a portion of hard, steely length.

He was velvety smooth, yet rigid as stone.

Lucky's fingertips pressed the underside in a fluttery caress.

His synapses exploded.

Kerreth shivered. Blinked. Came to his senses.

He put his hand firmly over hers to still her action.

"What-what are you doing?" she gasped, shocked.

"This isn't right, Red. We have to stop."

"What are you saying?"

"Now. Before it is too late and we both regret it."

"Huh?" Lucky gawked at him, dumbfounded. "Slick, have your circuits fried or something? We *have* to go on. And quickly at that!"

Kerreth took a deep breath. "Listen, I'm losing control and that is not a good sign–"

"It is a great sign! That is just what we are trying to do to you! Didn't you hear what Minmei said?"

His nostrils flared in annoyance and frustration. "I don't mean I'm losing *that kind* of control– I mean I'm losing *my* control!"

Crinkling her nose, Lucky grinned up at him rather impishly. "Wow. I didn't know I had it in me. Cool."

Despite (or because of) the insane situation, Kerreth pinched the bridge of his nose and chuckled. "Oh, I'd say you have a lot more than that going for you."

She beamed. "Really?"

"Really. But seriously, Red, there is something I have to tell you now, before we– Well, truthfully we can't. . . that is, we could, but you probably won't want to after I. . ."

Lucky rubbed her forehead. "Ugh! You're giving me a headache! Are all androids this chatty? Just say it so we can get on with it!" She paused to give him an appropriately wounded look. "You're killing my mood here, Slick."

"That's not a bad thing. Considering . . ." He took a deep breath and plowed on. "I can't go through with this. I *won't* go through with this."

"But-but why?"

He shrugged. "I don't feel right about it."

"*You don't feel right about it?*"

"No."

She had no idea what to say. He had completely flustered her. Was this some kind of shy program she was suppose to overcome? The big lug probably had all kinds of role-playing programs to initiate in different situations in order to please his endusers. No telling.

Once again– true to her name– she had spun the dice and come up with 'the reluctant school boy' sequence or something equally weirdo! At least she didn't get the mullethead construction worker program.

"Hey, aren't you designed to do this very thing, Slick? What is the big deal?"

" I am not designed to do this. In this way, at least." He tried to find an alternate excuse before putting his head in a tighter noose than it already was. "Listen, there is no. . . mood scenery. . . or . . . or. . ."

"Slick." She put her hands on her hips. "We don't have time for that. You're going to blow in-"

" *THIRTY-THREE POINT SEVEN MINUTES.*"

" No. I'm not. That's what I've been trying to tell you." He exhaled and decided to give it up to the *Sugarbabe*. "Please, don't get the wrong idea. I want you to know that I've enjoyed what we just did– I just can't go further in good conscience– which is really strange because I never knew I had a conscience when it came to this– which just goes to show that life is full of surp–"

Lucky snorted. "You are babbling. Minmei, could some of his functions be frying because we are getting close to critical radius?"

"AFFIRMATIVE. HE IS BECOMING IRRATIONAL AS THE CIRCUITS HEAT UP IN HIS GROIN."

"I am *not* becoming irrational! Listen to me; I am not a Masterstroke 6000! I am sorry to tell you this, but my name actually is–"

"HE IS TRYING TO REASSURE HIMSELF THAT HE IS STILL FUNCTIONING PROPERLY. POOR SLOWHAND-SAN. TEE-HEE-HEE. HIS AI IS STARTING TO CORRUPT AS A SIDE EFFECT OF REACHING CRITICAL RADIUS WHEN HIS PRIMAL FUNCTIONS WILL BE FULLY ENGAGED. PAY NO ATTENTION TO WHAT HE SAYS, MISS LUCKY. HE IS ALREADY IN COUNT DOWN MODE. YOU MUST ENFORCE HIS DIRECTIVE BY ANY MEANS. THERE IS THIRTY-TWO POINT TWO MINUTES UNTIL INITIATION SEQUENCE."

Kerreth rolled his eyes and shook his head no.

"Gotcha." She picked up a crazer and pointed it at his groin. "Strip' em. Or I'll start the stir-fry myself."

Kerreth gritted his teeth. "Are you not listening to me?!"

"Not any more. Lets go." She grabbed his hand and tugged him onto the bed. "We have to be quick now. No time for anything else."

"I am not doing this! That excuse for a computer doesn't know what its talking about! Where did you get that thing? At the Tonky Honk junkyards?"

Lucky's nostrils flared. It was one thing for her to insult Minmei– quite another for anyone who wasn't part of the crew.

"Just because she doesn't have all the bells and whistles doesn't mean she isn't good. She's- she's great!"

"THANK YOU, MISS LUCKY. I THINK YOU'RE GREAT TOO."

Kerreth slapped his forehead. They were all insane. "I am not going to make love to you. At least not like this."

"THERE IS NOW THIRTY MINUTES UNTIL DETONATION. I AM GOING INTO SELF-PRESERVATION MODE. TEE-HEE-HEE."

"Oh-oh."

"What?" Kerreth looked back and forth from Lucky to the ceiling from whence an invisible Minmei spoke. "What does she mean 'self-preservation mode'?"

"If you do not disengage, she's gonna blow us up herself."

"What the–!"

"I AM PROGRAMMED TO PROTECT LIFE WHENEVER POSSIBLE. THERE IS NOW A STRONG POSSIBILITY THAT YOUR GONAD DETONATION WILL AFFECT A NEARBY SPACE STATION ON WHICH 3.5 LIFE FORMS EXIST. I CANNOT ALLOW THAT TO HAPPEN. THEREFORE, I HAVE CALCULATED THAT I MUST MOVE YOUR POTENTIAL EXPLOSION SEQUENCE UP BY ONE MINUTE. THIS WILL ALLOW SUFFICIENT DISTANCE BETWEEN THE BLAST ZONE AND THE SPACE STATION TO ENSURE THE CONTINUATION OF THOSE LIFE FORMS."

Kerreth paled. "Is she saying what I think she's

saying?"

"Yeah. We just lost a minute in our quest to get you crazy in lust."

Kerreth ran his hands through his hair. "This cannot be happening."

"Well, it wouldn't be if you just went with the program."

He squinted at her. "What program is that?"

"Let's just say I'm not the one who has the nutnukes."

"Stop. That. Program. I am not–"

Minmei did not let him finish.

"I CANNOT, SLOWHAND-SAN. ONCE ENGAGED, THE PROGRAM CANNOT BE OVERRIDDEN UNLESS THE CONDITIONS TO ABORT HAVE BEEN MET."

"Meaning?"

"MEANING YOU MUST DIFFUSE YOUR OWN BOMB BY THE METHODS WE HAVE DESCRIBED FIRST."

"There isn't any bomb!" he shouted.

"THAT DOES NOT COMPUTE. I ASSURE YOU THERE IS A BOMB CONCEALED WITHIN YOUR TITANIUM CROTCH POCKET. THE FACT THAT YOUR AI IS UNAWARE OF THIS SEEMS TO BE A PART OF YOUR PROGRAMMING. THIS IS LOGICAL. IF THE MASTERSTROKES WERE TOLD OF THE FAILSAFE, THERE WOULD BE A HIGH PROBABILITY THAT SUCH KNOWLEDGE WOULD CREATE AN INTERNAL CONFLICT AND IMPEDE THEIR PERFORMANCE."

That smug, yet totally whacked computer was starting to really irritate him. "Look, Minmei, for the last time, I am not–"

"TIME TO INTERNAL BLAST IS TWENTY-FOUR POINT TWENTY-FIVE MINUTES. I AM LOCKED AND LOADED. PLEASE DO NOT

MAKE ME DESTROY MYSELF."

"Can she be talked out of this?"

"Nope."

"You sure?"

"It's a shtick."

He groaned.

"Look, can we at least agree to try to save the others on the ship and settle this. . . this delusion of yours later? We seemed to be enjoying ourselves before. Let's just give it our best and see what happens. It's all we can do."

He raised up on his elbows as she sat on the bed. "Do not even think to use calm reasoning on me when this entire ship belongs under the care of Dr. Boateh."

Dr. Boateh was a renowned psycho-realist who ran a famous mental institution on MukLuk. Lucky narrowed her eyes at him.

"So, you'll just let us die?"

He was beat and knew it.

In the strangest twist that had ever hit the sails of rogues anywhere, he was being forced to make love to a woman so his balls didn't explode.

After which, said woman– and/or her notorious brother– would kill him anyway.

If that didn't qualify for a bad day– he was not sure what did.

"Shit. C'mere." Kerreth grabbed her in armlock and tumbled over, stopping the roll with him on top.

"Just try and relax, Slick. But be sure to get excited at the same time." She gave him an encouraging nod.

He snorted. "Nothing like a little pressure on a guy."

His lean hips wriggled out of the rest of the jumpsuit.

"Remember, you're a masterstroke 6000. You can do this."

"Pride in the brand. Give me your mouth."

Lucky lifted her chin and misquoted SpinDrift who had misquoted another quote. "It is a far better thing you are about to do, then would be if you didn't do it at all."

He placed his hands on her shoulders. "That makes no sense."

She gave him a peculiar look. "You don't understand it?"

"Hey, the Masterstroke 6000 is knowledgeable in over 6000 ways to make love. You want understanding too?"

"Well, Ghandi also knew how to weave cloth."

"You're logic is very hard to follow."

"CAPTAIN ARROWS CLAIMS THE SAME."

"Butt out, Minmei!" Lucky snapped at the irksome computer.

"HIS TERM FOR ILLOGICAL IS WHACKED."

"Minmei!"

Kerreth threw back his head suddenly and roared with laughter at the absurdity of the entire situation. "You know, I can't remember when I've had this much fun." His dark golden eyes twinkled with mirth. "Listen, sweet Red, when you think of this– and you will– please be kind."

"THE TIME TO GONAD EXPLOSION IS TWENTY-TWO POINT FOUR MINUTES."

"You will enjoy yourself. I promise." While he wasn't sure he knew six thousand ways of making love, Kerreth was reasonably confident he knew *almost* that many.

In his line of work, it all came down to creativity.

Such creativity lent itself to many areas. If this gorgeous

redhead was willing to play out the script, he'd show her a great denouement.

So Kerreth began to make love to her as if his life depended on it.

And, of course, it did.

He wasted no time on gentle preliminaries. His plan of attack was to hit her senses with an all out assault.

He slid his leg between her thighs. The red curls at her juncture were damp from their prior kisses, but she wasn't nearly wet enough. *How much time did they have?*

A sheen of sweat dotted his brow.

Kerreth grabbed her ankles, flipped himself over, and proceeded to go down on her like no one had ever gone down on anyone in their lives. He swept his tongue over her in fast, long laps, licking up the juices that started to flow. With every sweep, he expertly flicked her clitoris.

With the first touch of his tongue, Lucky clenched his shoulders. Gasping in shock, she almost bolted off the bed. "Holy crap! Do you have to do *that*?" she squealed.

He raised his head slightly. "Do you want the whole package delivered or just the wrapping?" he intoned dryly.

"Um. . . but. . . *oh*!" He didn't wait for her response. His teeth scraped against her mound. She reeled off the bed again.

"Mmmm, you are delicious, Red." Kerreth was already stimulated by this sample of her. "I wish I had more time to do this."

His fingertips skimmed the rim of her earlobe, leaving intoxicating sensations in their wake. His other fingers glided alongside her nether lips, the caresses causing the same shivering bliss.

Lucky choked back a sob, caught between languor and out of control desire.

Swiftly, that scalding, caressing tongue thrust inside her and pushed deep. A slow, steady pulsing began throbbing from her inner core. Low levels at first; but soon building in strength and frequency until the waves crested over and over each other.

Lucky, who had never experienced anything remotely like this in her entire life, was now being handed the entire smorgasbord on one plate. She threw back her head and screamed her release.

"Oh, my gawd!!" Pause. *"Oh, my gawd!!"* Pause. *"Oh. My. GAWD!"*

Kerreth wasted no time.

Indeed he had no time to waste.

"IMPACT IS IN FOURTEEN MINUTES."

"I wish she'd stop with that! This is hard enough," he muttered to himself.

"It is?" came the small voice under him.

He looked down to see Lucky staring wide-eyed at his jutting erection.

He had always heard that he was well endowed but her awestruck reaction made him kind of uneasy. It was almost as if she. . . Nah. Couldn't be.

He was ready. She seemed more than ready. Flickerin' right; she was dripping all over him and it was heating him up fast. Maybe he was a sex android after all? She was sure makin him act like one.

He was thick and hard and howling for release.

He ran the tip of his erection along the moistened cleft. She was slick with dew. All he had to do was slip inside. The rest would take care of itself.

But she was probably not going to respect him in the morning.

Lucky knew he was close to completing the act with her. She swallowed and braced herself for the impact of his thrust.

He paused for an instant just before he entered her. "I'm sorry we have to do it like this, sweet Red."

Then he thrust.

Lucky screamed.

Stunned, Kerreth yelled out a garbled expletive. "*What the–?*"

He exhaled, horrified at what he had just discovered. Still buried inside her, he was hesitant to even move.

Lucky shut her eyes as tight as she could to stop the tears from falling. She didn't think it would hurt so much!

Kerreth began to sweat. He had been holding back more than she would ever know. After what he had just discovered, he wasn't sure he could continue on.

"I am sorry, Red; why didn't you say something?" His low-pitched voice was hushed. "I can't do this. . ."

"YOU HAVE LESS THAN TWELVE MINUTES TO ACHIEVE SHUT DOWN, SLOWHAND-SAN. PERHAPS I SHOULD SAY BUHBYE, SPACE COWBOYS?"

"We don't have time for cold feet! Hurry!" Lucky urged him on before Minmei blew them all to kingdom come.

"You're right; but I am going to make it up to you later."

"Let's hope there is a later." She smiled faintly at him.

"Now get on with it!"

He started to move in her. Very carefully and very gently. "Let me know if I'm hurting you."

Hurting her? He was perfect.

The initial stinging started to subside, leaving her to realize that Slick fit her like a glove and filled her to perfection. The sensation of him stroking inside was something she could get addicted to.

No wonder the Masterstrokes were so popular.

Who wouldn't want one of these guys stored under their beds?

She sighed blissfully.

Each stroke lengthened and quickened. Kerreth set up his rhythm and tried to bring her along with him. He covered her mouth with his kisses; he scraped her collarbone with little sweeps of his tongue; he captured the tips of her crested breasts with his teeth and pressed and suckled on them– all the while he never ceased his rhythmic thrusting.

The part of him that was inside her was trembling.

She could probably feel that.

He had to keep control to get this just right. He could not let her. . . He had to protect her; especially now.

Like most rogues, Kerreth had done many questionable things in his past. But on this day– for a woman he was just getting to know– he became a hero.

He swelled inside that velvety, wet canal. Swelled to bursting.

Still, he held himself back.

From what he understood, this had to be timed exactly

right or Minmei would take it upon herself to blast them into space dust.

Odd timing, but the outrageous humor of the situation got to him once again. Regardless of what transpired *something* was going to explode on the Sugarbabe. The next few seconds would determine what it would be: him or the entire ship.

He responded to the situation with raspy chuckle.

He thrust faster; ripples of pleasure filling both of them.

"EXPLOSION IN TEN. . . NINE. . . EIGHT. . ."

Kerreth took his cue. He stroked harder and swifter. Lucky began writhing under him. Moaning something about how good machines were. He started groaning in pleasure.

". . . SEVEN. . . SIX. . . FIVE . . ."

Losing just a bit of his control, he flexed inside her, hitting a secret erogenous zone. Lucky skyrocketed.

Her pulsing began at once. She screamed his name.

Well, the name she thought was his.

Kerreth huskily corrected her. "*Kerreth*, sweet." He ground his hips into her. "Kerreth."

"FOUR. . . THREE . . ."

He threw back his head and with a roar of pleasure, sank into the canal as deep as he could go.

"TWO. . ."

"Oh no!" Lucky wailed. "We're going to be too la-"

Kerreth hit critical mass. The explosion rocked Lucky. He gushed into her endlessly. A long, steady stream of a release. Like a hot shot of rapid fiery tingles.

Lucky shivered and thought she would start coming all over again. If the entire ship didn't explore first. Her insides quivered deliciously in response to him.

Following his valiant effort, Kerreth collapsed over her. *Were they dead?*

Minmei's voice wafted over them. "WE ARE NOW CLEAR OF THE SLIDE CRITICAL RADIUS. CONGRATULATIONS. YOU ARE A FREE ANDROID, SLOWHAND-SAN. SELF-DESTRUCT ABORTED."

"I am not an android, you wonky computer," he murmured against Lucky's damp neck.

"Don't be silly, Slick. No one but an android could come at will like that. Don't deny what you are– be proud!" Lucky stroked his dark golden hair. "You timed that perfectly– for which we are all eternally grateful."

Lucky liked him as an android?

He grinned against her neck. They had survived the impending explosion, his cover was apparently *still* good, and they were on their way to retrieve the Heart of the Merchandiser.

Not bad.

Best of all, he had just had truly incredible sex with a beautiful woman he had recently met. For a rogue like him, it simply didn't get any better than this.

He thought he'd store this memory away for one of those stormy nights when he thought of retiring from his present occupation.

On top of that, he was kind of wild about this woman.

He nibbled her satiny earlobe. "Mmmm, Red. . . now that the danger is over, we could do this again– only without the outside interference and pressure."

"Can't. Sorry." Lucky pushed Kerreth off her and sat up.

He was stunned. It was as if someone had given him a

taste of his favorite sweet, then taken the plate away permanently. "Why not?"

Lucky viewed him through half-lowered lids.

The man was gorgeously tousled– and he definitely had that sleepy, satisfied look that was altogether sexy as hell.

She didn't know whether to kill him or kiss him.

"*If* I do this with you again, *Slick,* I'd be tempted to *boss* you around a bit. I'm not sure you're *programmed* for that." She threw him a flippant look.

Lucky would boss him around? Kerreth immediately got hard again. "Ah, Red, you can boss me around in bed all you like. I'm aiming to please you, sweet." He winked at her.

She bit her lip. Okay, she was leaning towards kissing.

"You'd have to obey my every command; fulfill every one of my desires. What do you say to that?"

He tried not to groan aloud. Sounded like prime time to him. "I could do it."

"Hmmm. . ." She tapped her chin. "I suppose I *might* consider it– if you agree to *behave.*"

His heartbeat kicked up a notch. "Let me show you how well I can behave," he whispered huskily.

"Hmpf." Lucky crossed her arms over her chest. "Well, be quick about then! I haven't got all day."

"We'll see."

He smiled mysteriously as he covered her body with his own.

Lucky soon learned that certain Masterstrokes were not always *nice*.

But they were always *good*.

EPISODE SEVEN:
BOARDWALK FOR PARKPLACE

Onboard the Zoltarian pirate ship

As soon as Wildcat returned to Kokol's cabin, he realized that he had not underestimated his captor's potential.

She was already in contact with his ship.

The pirate was comfortably seated in front of her private communications console. No doubt pirate captains had some communications that they preferred to keep secret from their crew.

Wildcat had actually counted on that.

She glanced at him over her shoulder. "The plans have changed, my handsome tracker."

"How's that?"

"I have discovered that you operate from a ship known as the Sugarbabe. Using some undercorp contacts I have, I was able to obtain your ship's discreet call numbers."

"Why do I see what's coming?" he drawled with a tight smile.

"Tsk-tsk. Don't be upset, lover. Surely you didn't think I'd turn my back on the Heart of the Merchandiser simply because of our special friendship?"

"The thought tried to cross my mind but was quickly beaten to rational death."

She snickered. "Sensible *and* sexy. Who could ask for more?"

"I'm going to make a wild conjecture here and say. . . *you*?"

"Clever, too. How can I bring myself to toss you back?"

"Ah, let me see. . ." Wildcat crossed his arms over his chest. "A ransom should do it."

"Precisely."

"Mmm. So I reckon we're through over there?" He nodded towards the mussed up bed.

"For the time being."

"And here I cleaned up all nice and pretty for you."

She sniffed at him. "The disinfectant has not eradicated your glorious natural scent. It makes me hungry just sampling it! Perhaps I will make use of you once more after all." She rested her chin in her palm.

Wildcat was not so amenable. "Perhaps *not*. We had a deal, Captain. Can't have it both ways."

She laughed. "Of course I can. I am a pirate– that is what pirates do. We have it both ways. . . to our liking."

Wildcat shrugged. "Gotta admire the attitude if not the fair play."

"Be a good captive– come and stand by me so your crew can see I actually have the goods."

He smoothly moseyed over to where she was seated.

"Perfect. Simply grin and bear it, my Wildcat. It should all be over in a few moments."

"I'll just think of England," he murmured wryly.

"What was that?"

"I said I'll just relax." He gave her a sexy grin. "They say it makes it easier."

She snorted. "Don't be so dramatic! Remember what the corporations say: it's not personal."

"Well, that makes me feel a whole lot better."

Ignoring his sarcasm, she punched in the Sugarbabe's discreet call numbers.

***

Onboard the Sugarbabe

"Incoming!!!"

SpinDrift's not so soothing voice flickered into Lucky's consciousness.

She rustled the covers.

"What is it?" A deep, husky voice played with her senses.

Lucky tried to compose herself. It wasn't easy after that last experience with him. Piloting a space ship as a kid wasn't nearly as much fun. Slick took gaming to a whole new level. The Playstation XXI had nothing on him.

"It's SpinDrift. Someone's trying to contact the ship. I better get up on deck."

She started to rise.

A strong arm went around her waist forestalling her.

Kerreth gently nibbled across her earlobe. "Can't the Floop get it?" To punctuate his suggestion, his sleep-warmed lips placed tiny, honey kisses along her collarbone.

"We're talking about SpinDrift. Sure, he can take a message– but you'll never be positive what was actually *said*. Besides, it could be that Heiner guy about the miadne. I should check it out."

"Good point, I suppose." He lifted his arm, releasing her. "I'll go with you."

"It's not necessary. You can stay here; I'll be back in a few." Lucky's facial expression let it be known she was not finished with her personal Masterstroke yet.

Kerreth held his groan in check.

He hated to admit to his masculine pride that he was close to being worn out. And by an inexperienced lover! Lucky Red was a wild and adventuresome package of grade A trouble.

And he had the sweetest time with her. . .

That was the problem.

Kerreth furrowed his brow. He really didn't want her to believe the truth– it would ruin everything between them.

For suck's sake! He was sort of *fancying* her.

A lot.

This was a totally new predicament for him. As far as she was concerned he was just an android. A favored android, true. But still an android.

So how long could he keep this up?

Kerreth viewed her from under lowered lids. She had made it clear. *He had to perform for her or he would be history.*

He did not want to be history.

Sure, he might have a stake in the gem but along the way he had found something better. *A real treasure.*

One he didn't intend to lose.

Every thief, saboteur, dealmaker, and wheeler-dealer from here to Volauvent was after the Heart of the Merchandiser. The Sugarbabe was ahead of the pack. Just. Because of this, Lucky had become an unwitting target.

He was not letting her out of his sight until he knew she was safe and that gem was safely in his possession. When the time was right he would explain everything to her.

Until then he was going to be her private pleasure machine.

Even if it killed him.

He was going to enjoy this 'treasure' as long as he could. As far as that incoming message– he had to hear it. He quickly sat up and grabbed his uniform. "I'll go with you, Lucky."

"It's really not necessary, Slick."

Yes, it was.

"I can be of help. You might need me."

Lucky shrugged. "Suit yourself."

On the way to the bridge it crossed Lucky's mind that for an android Slick Slowhand was terrible at taking orders.

Maybe it's part of the Masterstroke's protocol? A built in uber-male code or something?

It did make him sexier, she acknowledged.

But only because it's not for real. *I certainly wouldn't want a man behaving like that.*

Too alpha.

* * *

When she got to the bridge, SpinDrift was trying to hold off the poor messenger with little success.

"I demand to speak to whoever is in charge at once!" came the irritated bark through the console.

Lucky turned to Kerreth. "What did I tell you? I love Spin dearly, but he lacks certain people skills."

"You mean he is irritating."

"I wouldn't say that," Lucky defended her friend. "He's . . . well, he. . . he has a certain . . ."

Kerreth viewed her askance. "Hummm?"

"He's extremely creative!" she snapped, storming away. "What's up, Spin?"

"Oh! Thank goodness you're here! This is the rudest, most impossible person I have ever–"

"Captain Kokol from the Zoltarian ship, *Bobone,* and I am not pleased–"

Lucky interrupted the peevish tirade.

"This is Lucky Arrows. What can I do for you, Captain?"

"What kind of a ship are you running?! I have been trying to contact you for over–"

"I was indisposed. Please state your business." Unapologetic , Lucky couldn't imagine what a Zoltarian would want with the Sugarbabe.

Kerreth flicked off the communications switch before she had a chance to say anything else.

Lucky gave the android a less than patient look.

"Just because we slept together, do not presume to overstep your position on board this ship." She sternly addressed him.

Kerreth, of course, got hard again. *Call me sick, but I'm lovin' this.* He was very close to asking her if she intended to give him a spanking later. Instead, he tried to keep his mind on the situation at hand.

"Most Zoltarians are pirates, Red. I thought you should know that before continuing the conversation. Be wary of everything she says and do not trust her. Whatever she wants, I can guarantee it will not be to your benefit."

"Got it." Lucky tried to open the link.

Kerreth forestalled her once more.

"I mean it, Red; these pirates can be dangerous to tangle with. Whatever you do do not agree to any terms with them until you think it through."

Lucky nodded. "Okay. *Got it.*"

She sat down and instructed Minmei to open her visual connection. "Okay, what can we do for–"

She stopped in mid sentence. Her *brother* was standing behind and to the left of the pirate captain!

"*Wildcat!*" she gasped.

"Sensei Wildcat?!" The Floop almost fell over his big webbed feet as he waddled over as quickly as he could.

"GREETINGS, CAPTAIN." Minmei addressed their skookum tumtum leader directly.

"Urrr!" Clugot chimed in from the lower deck. He was monitoring the call from the cargo bay. It made Lucky feel good that the engineer was trying to look out for them in his own way. Kelvinators were sometimes like that.

"Greetings Minmei, Lucky. . . *all* of you." His eyes narrowed as he caught sight of the fluttering Floop on deck.

Lucky noticed her brother's aquiline nostrils flare in annoyance– but she could tell he was happy to see Spin, too.

The tracker was exactly what Kerreth expected.

He looked tough and savvy. A real brawler.

Which probably did not bode well for the faux Masterstroke 6000 that had slept with his sister.

Make that innocent sister.

I'm a dead man. Kerreth took a deep breath and slowly exhaled it.

Lucky examined her brother's appearance. He looked a little tired from his ordeal, but not bad considering everything he must have been through. Wildcat was still as gorgeous as sin.

"Where are you?!" She was overjoyed to finally hear his voice. "We were so worried! I can't believe you're finally–"

Behind the Zoltarian, her brother jerked his thumb across his throat, warning her to be silent.

Apparently, she was giving away too much already.

She sneaked a peek at Slick, but he was focused on the Cat.

"I see by your enthusiasm that you wish your comrade's safe return. How heartwarming." Captain Kokol grinned at her. "And how fortuitous for us that you care so much for the state of his handsome hide."

Lucky had the distinct impression the grin was not an 'I'm so happy for you ' smile at all.

"What's going on?" Lucky asked the woman, warily.

"It is simple. We have your Captain, as you can plainly

see. If you wish him back it will cost you."

"Cost me? How do you mean?"

"*Ransom,* my dear. We are pirates. We like to get paid for our troubles. Look it up– you'll see it is true."

Lucky gasped. "You *kidnapped* him?"

The Zoltarian brushed her hand back and forth as if the suggestion was utterly ridiculous. "Kidnapping is illegal, my dear. We *rescued* him. All we ask is that we simply be paid *in kind* for our kind deed."

"Or else what?"

Wildcat shook his head, but she had already asked the question. Besides, no gain, no foul.

"Or else we shall dispose of him, I suppose."

Okay, that was fairly foul. Her shoulders sagged. "You'd kill my brother?"

Two groans hit her simultaneously.

One from the screen and other from behind her.

"Ah, so this is your *brother*. Well, well, well. That changes everything. The price of his release must reflect his worth to you, true? We Zoltarians cannot have you accuse us of a direct insult to the value of your family."

Wildcat slapped his forehead with the heel of his hand. "Elle le descendra avant qu'il nage!"

Lucky bit her lip. Her brother was muttering in french under his breath. That was *never* good.

Minmei helpfully translated the first part of his tirade.

"SHE SINKS IT BEFORE IT SWIMS!"

Lucky turned red. Okay, so she sucked at playing poker.

She was sure she caught her name being mentioned by her brother once or twice between the ensuing 'merdes' too. If he started in on the latin she might as well leave him to his fate. She knew from experience at that point it was all over.

Wildcat only uttered latin during two moods. Neither of which were pretty.

"Be careful what you say." Kerreth hissed the warning from the sidelines.

A bit late, if you asked her.

"I. . . um . . ."

Fortunately Lucky was saved from having to continue the conversation with Kokol because another call light flashed up on the panel.

"Incoming two!" SpinDrift merrily rang out.

Lucky rolled her eyes. That Floop only lived for the mad hijinks that played out onboard this ship!

"Ah, could you excuse me for a moment, Captain Kokol? I have another call coming in."

"Wait!"

That was her brother.

He seemed to almost lunge at the screen as she clicked off to take the other call. *What was his problem?*

Kerreth pinched the bridge of his nose. "Ah, do you think it wise to put kidnappers on hold, Red?"

"Oh, they'll wait." Lucky was not worried about losing pirates. "The Zoltarians went to a lot of trouble to find us. Believe me, they're not about to disconnect our link. There would be no profit in it for them."

"Hope your right. Your brother's life may depend on it."

"I'm right." She crossed her fingers anyway. *Good grief! How had Wildcat gone and gotten himself kidnapped?*

And by Zoltarians no less!

They were not noted for being an especially cordial group. A Zoltarian had once killed a man in a tavern for mispronouncing the name of his favorite grog!

No apology given.

Well, she would deal with them later. Right now she had to take care of this other call.

Taking a deep breath, she opened the incoming communication link, leaving the visual off.

"Arrows, is that you?!" Heiner's scratchy voice bleated through the old speakers.

Lucky broke into a sweat. She didn't have that stupid stone and she knew the Volauventian was getting antsy.

Still, they had found what they hoped was a clue to the jewel's possible whereabouts. Maybe. Kind of.

"Yes," she sighed. "Go ahead, Mr. Heiner."

"Have you found the Heart of the Merchandiser yet?"

No beating around the bush with this guy. "Well, I–"

"Time is growing short, Arrows!"

Why did she just know he was going to say that?

And why does no one ever worry if time grows long? It couldn't *always* be a good thing, could it?[10]

"We haven't found the jewel, Mr. Heiner– but we have found a good lead." She caught SpinDrift's eye.

The Floop had an expression that said it was news to him.

Heiner got excited right away. "What kind of lead?"

"Well, we found a chip on Slide that we believe will

---

[10] Yes, it could, as proven by Doraxparralax of the Dustbin stellar grouping over a millennium ago in his theory of incongruous dawdling. Time growing long is always good.

lead us directly to the stone."

A huge blast of disgusted exhale blared through the speakers. Both Lucky and Spin jumped back.

"*What does that mean?!* Speak in plain terms!!"

"Umm. . . well. . . the chip. . ."

Lucky wasn't sure if telling him that the chip yielded a minute sampling of a fiber– and that they were tracking back to that fiber's origin point– would sound as if they had lost their minds. There was no way of knowing whether that fiber was actually associated with the jewel, but it was their only lead.

Kerreth stepped forward. "Just tell him that there was information encoded on the chip that you were able to break down," he whispered. "Tell him that you believe that the Heart of the Merchandiser has been taken to Dumfug 8."

Lucky muted the link. "What if we don't find it there?"

"It's a start and it sounds as if his patience is running out. You don't want to loose the finder's fee, do you?"

"No, you're right." She flipped off the mute. "We are enroute to Dumfug 8 as we speak, Heiner. We're planning to dock above Port Royal 4. "

"Excellent! Sounds like you have almost solved the case, Arrows!"

Lucky blanched. "Well, I wouldn't say–"

"Congratulations. We will meet there to help you retrieve the jewel and to give you your just reward!"

"We?"

"Big Gun, himself, is coming to collect what is his. Wait for us outside the city limits, behind the dock-link station."

"But–"

"Heiner out."

Lucky cringed. If they did not find that jewel Big Gun would have them all for lunch.

Just when had this day gone bad?

Oh, yeah. When she woke up.

"Well, we don't have any idea where that stupid stone is and Big Gun, himself, is meeting us right by the dock-link. Can this get worse, people?"

Kerreth nodded. "Ah, brother still on hold. . . kidnapping. . . Ring a bell, Red?"

"Oh, crap!" Lucky dove for the audio/visual connection. "Captain Kokol, are you still there?"

"Yes, I am." came the choppy response. "That delay is going to cost you." Her scowling puss filled the screen.

"Geesh, is there anything you don't charge extra for?"

The Zoltarian's lips curved into wry amusement. "Don't be cheeky. Or it will cost you."

Her brother snorted.

Some victim, Lucky fumed. Her brother seemed a bit too familiar with this captor of his. There was no telling how he got caught in this predicament in the first place.

Although, knowing him, he probably arranged it somehow.

Bro, you are usually a naughty devil, so I had better assume you did arrange this and go from there.

"All right, Captain," Lucky yawned and stretched her arms. "Let's get to the terms. What do you want for the scoundrel?"

Kokol grinned, showing her pointed incisors. "I like you,

redheaded woman. But he won't come easy."

SpinDrift flicked his pointed spurs at the screen. "From what I hear, Sensei Arrows never does."

The Zoltarian captain frowned at the Floop.

Before the pirate could up the price yet again, Lucky quickly interjected, "Yes, we know that it's going to cost us. You've made that patently clear. So what are we talking about? What is it going to take to get my brother back?"

Kerreth rubbed the back of his neck as he faced the truth. He had recently discovered he was crazy about this woman; however, he had to be honest with himself. She totally lacked negotiation skills.

The way Red was going about it, she would be fortunate to see her brother again. Alive or otherwise.

And that was not something he could allow.

The trail was clear; he needed Arrows, the elder, to get to the Heart of the Merchandiser. "Get some assurance from her that he won't be harmed before you agree to anything."

She thought it over and agreed with him.

Actually, Lucky was glad Slick had come up on deck. Despite her initial misgivings, the Masterstroke 6000 was proving himself an asset to the entire crew.

"If you give me what I want, your brother will be freed. Alive and robust as always." Kokol assured her. "Now let's get down to it, shall we?"

"Go on."

"There is a certain *item* that has gone missing from one of the major corporations. . . I think you know what I am referring to."

Lucky's jaw dropped. "How do you know about the Heart osf the Merchandiser?"

The two stereo groans buffeted her again. Wildcat and Slick.

What Lucky didn't realize was that both men were seeing that gorgeous hunk of rock known as the Heart of the Merchandiser slipping away from them.

Wildcat stepped forward and yelled at his sister, seemingly straight across the void of space. "You just let that out without waiting to see if that was what she was talking about? I can't believe it!"

Lucky was unapologetic. "Don't be such an ass, bro, of course that's what she meant."

She looked at the Zoltarian pirate. "Wasn't it?"

Kokol grinned from pointed ear to pointed ear. "Naturally."

Her brother didn't seem too happy with the affirmation.

Those narrowed eyes of his were impaling her with shards of icy blue fire. Such a stare carried with it the genetic force of countless warriors and chieftains.

Under its potent will, most people began quivering right where they stood.

It had no effect whatsoever on Lucky.

What was he so upset for anyway?

She wasn't the one who had gotten herself shanghaied! Now it was up to her to clean up this mess.

Lucky narrowed her eyes in a fair imitation of him, sending the volley back.

After all, she had been practising it with him her whole life. Didn't the big galoot realize he was in mortal danger?

What was some stupid stone compared to that?

"How do I know you won't kill all of us after you get what you want, Captain?" If they were going to do the trade, she needed more assurances than what she had heard so far. Wildcat's life was at stake. Maybe all their lives.

Kokol seemed amused by her stance.

"I am a pirate, sweetling. Despite what many believe, a good deal of the time we make our living through negotiations. It wouldn't go well for me if it got around the cosmos that I could not be trusted to stick to a deal by living up to my side of the bargain."

Yeah, but what if it all went wrong somehow?

This was tricky.

Lucky glanced up at the screen in time to see a glittering diaphanous film float by the captain's right shoulder.

In a flash, it disappeared.

Cloud.

Lucky blinked. So that's where that Auran had gotten himself to!

He had vanished from the ship soon after her brother's disappearance. Since no one but Wildcat knew of Cloud's comings and goings, his absence wasn't noticed right away.

Recently, though, the entire crew had begun to worry that something had happened to the mysterious assassin as well.

The Auran was letting her know that he was alongside Wildcat.

Good.

Having a deadly twilight assassin there to protect her

brother made her feel a lot better. Lucky discretely nodded at the screen to let Cloud know she had received his message.

A tear lodged in the corner of her eye.

She had never realized how utterly loyal the entire crew was to Wildcat.

"What was that?" Fearing some kind of Zoltarian trick, Kerreth approached the screen, placing himself in full view for the first time during the interaction with the pirates. "Did you see it, Red?"

Lucky winced. The last thing she wanted to do was alert the pirates to the fact that they had a dreaded Auran assassin onboard. They would positively freak. "Shh!"

She needn't have worried.

Upon seeing Kerreth, the Zoltarian Captain let out a shriek of the kind that is only uttered when a collector sees a longed-for collectable.

"GAGHHH! That- that uniform! That face! That perfect body!!" Kokol's eyes bugged out. "Is- is he a-a–" She swallowed almost too excited to dare speak its name. "Could that. . . *Could that be a Masterstroke 6000?"*

"Wha?" Lucky glanced from the screen to Slick.

Her android was dressed once again in his jumpsuit from Slide.

The jumpsuit that delineated every muscular bulge on his hunk self. *The jumpsuit that clearly stated his performance name over the breast pocket area.*

Damn! There was no denying it now.

Why did Slick have to get in that pirate's face? This was not going to be cool. "Ah, so what if he is?"

Kokol had an immediate choking fit.

Wildcat patted her back. Patiently. Maybe a bit too forcefully. *Thwap.* Whap. *Thwap.* Whap.

"Enough!" She grabbed his hand to stop the backslaps.

While Kokol recovered, Wildcat locked eyes with his sister. A steely-eyed stare that sent bullets of blue in a riveting, paralyzing attack.

Okay, so *that* look made her a teensy bit nervous.

She swallowed.

"Lucky." He drew her name out in a low, long tone.

"Um, yes, brother?" she answered in a small voice.

His speech level dropped some more, becoming very soft. "What in the hell is that *thing* doing on my ship. . ."

Didn't seem like a question that expected an unreasonable answer.

So Lucky wisely didn't answer.

The Zoltarian Captain put her hand on her brother's arm to calm him down. "Never mind that, Cat– how did she get it?"

The Zoltarian and her brother started to carry out their own little conversation, so there really was no need for her to get involved. Lucky almost started whistling under her breath as the two of them went back and forth.

"Half of Crisyn will be hunting for me!" Her brother roared.

"They are impossible to steal! It-it must be priceless!" Kokol squealed. Then the pirate's eyes gleamed as the reality of what she had just said sank in.

Wildcat summed up his reaction in one. *"Shit."*

Kerreth waited for his sentence to fall– the one that was

going to permanently mess up his future.

He was going to have to come clean. Right now.

And *that* was sure to land him in even more trouble.

The Zoltarian pirate would want to toss him overboard into deep space for getting her hopes up. The Floop would be disappointed the fun was over. Minmei would use the opportunity to lobby for better sensors. Clugot would voice his displeasure with an *ur.* Lucky would be furious and terribly hurt.

And the elder Arrows. . .

Ah, yes, the brother that looked like a savage warrior chieftain from Earth's past. . . *He* would most likely throttle him after what he had done to his sister.

Kerreth surreptitiously eyed Wildcat. Could he take him in a fight?

By the size of that clenched fist. . . Probably not.

Self-preservation demanded he remain silent as long as he could.

Kokol was first to assert her professional rights to him. "I want him!" she announced straightaway.

That's number one. Kerreth began to count off his future headaches as they all tried to hop aboard the Masterstroke excursion.

Meanwhile, Lucky was nonplussed at Kokol's proprietary attitude. As far as she was concerned, Slick was not part of the bargain. "Well, you can't have him! He's mine, so forget it."

Two. Kerreth knew Lucky was going to hate him for his ruse. He still didn't want to leave her.

Wildcat stared at his sister and then stared at Kerreth.

And back and forth once more.

As if to be sure of what he was seeing.

He was ominously silent.

That makes three. Kerreth acknowledged that this last one was definitely the most dangerous of the lot.

SpinDrift suddenly pulled up a seat, unwrapped a pocketed snack, and settled himself in for the delicious entertainment. "Oh, this is flawless!"

The Zoltarian pirate shot the first salvo straight across Lucky's bow. "He's isn't yours. If you wish to see your brother alive again, you will hand him over to me!" Like any good pirate, Kokol paused to let her threat sink in.

Lucky's eyes became suspiciously moist.

This couldn't be happening! How could she give Slick up when she just found him? It was rather foolish, but she was *fond* of the 6000. He had been so sweet to her when they. . . No!

Just the thought of that-that *woman* using him made her feel nauseous. *Bleck*!

So she tried to stall Kokol.

"You can't mean it, Captain Kokol! You don't really want him; he's a corrupt unit. He'll put your ship in jeopardy for sure!"

Kokol waved Lucky's warning away. "My ship is always in jeopardy."

"But he's- he's *corporate!*" The ugliest word to any pirate.

"Surely not through and through, my dear?"

Lucky blushed.

"Some risks are worth taking and *he* looks to be a prize

worth fighting for. I've heard all about these special pleasure droids. It's enough to make a woman's mouth water!"

Lucky tried bluffing. "I am telling you, there is not much difference between the 6000s and the earlier 2000s. Same stroking techniques. Same conversational qualities. Okay, so he's *capable* of doing more– but where's the software support from third parties? It's all Crisyn hype! Next Gen bs. They only want to get the market hot– that's where it's at. You know the early performance holos?"

"I've seen them; yes."

"Not live action. Composites."

Kokol sucked in her breath. "No way."

"It's the truth. Didn't you ask yourself: how can he possibly be this *good*? Of course you did. We all did. It's just another marketing ploy to get us women to spend more money."

"I don't care!" Kokol's dreamy voice became reverent as she uttered the robot's design tag. *"I've longed for a 6000.* When they banned them from leaving Slide and supply went short, I thought I'd die until I got my hands on one."

Wildcat stared at the pirate captain agog. He didn't believe what he was hearing. What was it with women and these Masterstrokes? Plenty of men he knew said they couldn't get their women to stop playing with them; especially when new role-playing software came out.

The latest craze was some erotic vampire fantasy. Who knew what was next? Magical Knights? Lords of Sex? Where would it end?

"I'm completely crushed by this," he drawled, teasingly.

Kokol patted his firm thigh. "Don't take it personally, Cat. You are a magnificent lover. But a 6000!! I always prayed that one day I might come across one. It's a true rogue's fantasy! To enjoy the booty of the booty and still have it increase in value." She lowered her lashes demurely.

"If I live forever, I will never understand women." Wildcat remarked drolly as he observed her kittenish demeanor.

A whisp of a chortle tickled the atmosphere.

Wildcat snorted softly.

"I thought you said you wanted the Heart of the Merchandiser in exchange for Wildcat?" Lucky was still trying to hold firm against Kokol as they haggled over her brother's future.

Kokol perked up at the mention of the famous jewel. "Do you actually have the miadne stone?"

"Um, not yet."

Kokol folded her arms across her ample chest. "Then I want the android! Actually, I want the android anyway. At this point, he is nonnegotiable."

Lucky switched off the sound and turned regrettably to Kerreth. "I think I'm going to have to agree to this, Slick. I can't budge her. I can't help it; I have no other choice."

"You can't be serious, Red. We have a. . . a history going."

That sounded lame even to him. He looked at the screen and grimaced as Kokol ran her tongue over her pointed teeth.

He shuddered. He really hated that *thing* Zoltarians

did with their teeth! "I don't want to go with her."

"I'm sorry, Slick. I do like you. . . as a. . . peripheral device, but this is my brother's life we're talking about. There's nothing I can do. Once we switch for him, we'll see if we can get you back again."

Kerreth was not going with the Zoltarians. No. No. No.

Once the pirates realized they'd been swindled, they'd kill him in a nanosecond and then come straight after the Sugarbabe and its entire crew.

He could not let that happen.

Lucky had been innocent in more ways than one; she didn't know everyone was after the Heart of the Merchandiser. He had talked his way onto this ship; he couldn't put them in mortal danger because of it.

"Red, you can't do this trade. There is something I have to–"

"Please don't make this harder, Slick." She blocked him out and flipped the mute off before she could change her mind. "Okay, Captain Kokol. I'll agree to your terms."

"Wait!" Kerreth tried to stop her; but it was already a done deal.

"Excellent!" Pleased, the Captain sat back in her chair. "There is one more minor thing. . ."

"I told you not to trust her."

"Yes?"

"I still want the Heart of the Merchandiser."

"What?" Lucky gasped.

Wildcat spoke up. An android was one thing; the jewel was something else. "Don't you think you're getting enough as it is, Kokol, my darling cutthroat? I just hitched a little ride, after all."

She laughed. "Enough will be enough when it is enough."

Her response befuddled SpinDrift's Floop brain. *"Bra-aak!"* His half-eaten snack fell out of his claw.

Lucky had had enough. "Heart of the Merchandiser? Ugh! I have no idea where that stupid thing is! I'm starting to wish I never heard of it."

"Don't play coy with me."

All humor suddenly gone, the female pirate extended the nail of her index finger. The lethal-looking talon pressed immediately against her brother's throat, right above the carotid artery.

She at least warned Lucky. "One slice will be all it will take."

Wildcat was not loving this turn of events. He spoke in a calm, yet deadly voice. "This is not very neighborly of you, Kokol. I won't like you as much if you slice my throat."

"While I admire your pluck, Cat, you should remember that I can keep you alive while still delivering a considerable amount of damage. Your sister would still pay to get you back; you just wouldn't be in such good shape."

She pressed her nail along the skin of his throat. A bead of blood bubbled up.

Wildcat's eyes locked with the Zoltarian. "And here I thought you cared, Kokol."

"It's just business, lover."

Lucky clenched her fists. The last thing any of them wanted was for Wildcat to get hurt. "What should I do, Cat?" she cried to her brother. "I can't give her what I don't have."

Wildcat decided to challenge the pirate's greed. "Tell her the deal is off."

"No!" Lucky screamed.

Kerreth leaned over and whispered in her ear. "Tell her you'll meet her on Dumfug 8 and you'll do the exchange there."

"What good will that do?" she whispered back.

"It will give us a chance to come up with a plan. Tell her you'll hand me over to her at that time as well."

Lucky met Kerreth's gaze and her eyes filled with tears. "It's only for awhile; I promise we will get you back someday. I'm sorry to have to-" she swallowed. "To give you up, Slick."

"You won't get rid of me that easy, Red." He squeezed her hand.

"I'll- I'll give you what you want, Captain. Just don't hurt him! We'll meet you on Dumfug 8 and exchange as agreed."

The Zoltarian captain removed her talon from Wildcat's neck and clapped her hands. "What a happy day! 'Til we meet on Dumfug, then. It was a pleasure doing business with you, Lucky Arrows. Kokol out."

Just before the screen went black Lucky got a quick glimpse of the Auran assassin wafting over the Zoltarian Captain.

He was pulsing a rather menacing purple and red color.

Cloud could take that pirate out before she even knew what hit her. It was a highly unusual situation, but the Auran would never let Wildcat get hurt. She was sure of it.

All was not lost yet.

"Clugot?"

"Urrr?"

"Get us to Dumfug 8 as fast as you can. I don't think that woman has much patience."

"Ur."

"And thanks for sticking by us."

"Urr. Urr."

Lucky spun around in her chair. "Well, Spin we're off on the road to Dumfug 8." She tried to smile, but couldn't.

Seeing her downcast features, Kerreth whispered, "We still have a little time, Red. Would you like to go. . . rest?" He winked smartly at her.

"We don't have enough time, Slick. We'll be there shortly." She looked down. "I'm sorry."

"We have time." He took her hand and led her from the bridge.

". . . ooooh, we're off on the road to–" SpinDrift stopped singing and looked up as he realized he was all alone on the bridge. He put his claws on his hips.

"Well, this situation doesn't seem all that dire to me," he announced. "Lucky has found someone to play with at last. And Sensei Arrows just might have a new crew member!"

"Ur." Clugot quickly disconnected himself from the bridge. The screen went blank with a *blip*. Kelvinators subscribed to a keen concept of self-preservation: Never Engage The Floop.

"Hmf!" SpinDrift adopted his famous Belgian's accent. *"It is my weakness, it has always been my weakness, to desire to show off!"*

With that, he shook his feathered tail at the now dark screen and continued to sing old road songs as he danced across the floor, confident that all would be well.

* * *

Meanwhile on Planet Volauvent. . .

"I believe you are right, sir."

"I'm always right. That's why I am who I am."

"Of course, your superordinate one." Heiner clicked his heels. "It was sheer genius to place that message tap on them. How did you ever obtain that tech? I thought it was illegal for everyone but the Incomparable Honcho."

"Oh, it is. Except for one small technicality."

"And that is?"

"Whatnot developed the initial protocol." Big Gun had the nerve to grin.

Heiner tittered behind his hand. "Do you believe Wildcat was taken by the Zoltarians?"

"Sure. Do." Big Gun guffawed.

"It was odd, sir; for a moment I thought I saw the strangest flicker in the transmission. . ."

"Never mind that. These parallel compressions are never one hundred percent. Did you tell the girl to come straightaway to the dock-link to collect her reward?"

"Yes, I did."

"Good. We'll need to keep her hostage. Is that clear?"

"Perfectly. What about the Floop?"

"Please. You're killing me here."

EPISODE EIGHT: STARDUST

When they got back to the cabin, Lucky immediately threw off her clothes. "Well, what are you waiting for?"

Kerreth crossed his arms over his chest. "You know there is such a thing as foreplay, dearest."

"Don't be silly. I don't need that."

His eyes widened. "You don't need– !" He shook his head to clear the 'red' fuzz out. "Do you know what you're saying?"

"Uh-huh. I'm ready to go. *Really*." She gave him a sincere look and batted her lashes.

Kerreth swallowed. A sheen of sweat broke out across his forehead. She was making him uncomfortably *warm*. "Look, Red, I appreciate the enthusiasm, but it really isn't wise to jump into–"

She planted herself in front of him.

"I once read this book were the man– a shapechanger, if I recall– stood behind the woman and. . . Well, it was incredibly erotic."

She tapped her chin. "I think I'd like to try that."

Kerreth's eyes glazed over.

"I don't think that's wise. You're probably too sore to do–"

"I'll decide that."

"Red, you–"

"Get behind me, mister!" She smiled wickedly.

A part of Kerreth immediately assumed the rock hard position. *What was going on?* Every time that redheaded woman opened her mouth and that sweet melodious voice issued forth and *ordered* him about, he thought was going to erupt like a volcano.

He threw off his clothing.

"That's better." She examined him from head to toe.

No way he could hide the fact that he was already erect. So she had it in mind to take advantage of her Masterstroke, did she?

"Fine, Red, but you should be careful what you wish for."

He came up behind her and pulled her back against him.

Lucky gasped as she felt the velvety length of him slide against her buttocks. "Do you like that?" he breathed into her ear.

"Yes." She closed her eyes as his tongue followed the curves of her ear. Sharp teeth captured the delicate lobe, tugging sensuously.

"Mmmm. Keep going, Slick. This is great."

"As you wish." His arms came around her waist to clasp her to him.

Lucky realized his skin was scorching hot wherever they touched. It was simply perfect–

Until the ship's climate control took that precise opportunity to send a blast of cold air down from the ceiling right onto her. She jumped.

"Yikes! What is wrong with this wacko ship?!" Lucky paused. "Wait, that actually feels good. No thanks to that doof of a computer!"

"Mmmm, that does feels nice," Slick whispered. "Makes me think of the cool island breezes on Grenaday Bay Colony."

"Have you been there?"

"Of c-" Kerreth caught himself. As an android who supposedly never left Slide, he couldn't have been there. "Of course not. I have imagined it, though."

"When you make love?" Lucky lifted her chin, not at all sure she wanted to hear about his past exploits of making love with endless amounts of women.

Kerreth kissed the side of her neck. "Just with you," he answered diplomatically.

"They really do take extra care with your programming. Well said."

He smiled. His palm caressed the side of her ribcage as his mouth continued to play along the edge of her throat. "I doubt I have been with as many women as most Masterstrokes. You, ah, caught me relatively early in my *sexbot* career." He grinned into her neck.

"Very funny."

"I try to please." He nipped her shoulder.

"Good; that's exactly the response I expected of you– even though you are far too skilled for me to think otherwise."

"My skill doesn't come from experience; remember?"

Her face colored. "I-I know that. I just think that someone who is so well *programmed* wouldn't be left 'unused' for very long."

He stilled and lifted an eyebrow. "I'm not sure I care for the way you phrased that."

"I didn't mean it as an insult! One should take pride in excellence of any kind."

"Uh-huh."

Lucky sighed. "Seriously. You know what?" She turned halfway in his arms and looked over her shoulder at him.

"What's that?" He hugged her.

"I'd be happy to give you an endorsement for future reference!"

Kerreth coughed. "That's, uh, good of you, Lucky. But I think I'll be looking for a different line of work. So tell me, what excited you about this love scene you read?" He palmed her breast and flicked the tip with his thumb.

The peaks of both her breasts hardened into jutting nubs.

"It was the way he took her. Passionately. Wildly. He was focused only on her. He gave himself completely over to his passion."

"Ah."

"Have you ever done that?" Her head fell back against his shoulder.

"No one ever expected it of me," he said quietly.

"I guess I'll be the first; just as you were mine."

His heart thumped. "What did I tell you, Red . ." His breath skittered along her collarbone as he caressed her lovingly with his hands and body. "Be careful what you wish for."

"I'm hardly worried. You are bound to do anything I ask of you."

"Am I?" He wedged his thigh between her legs.

Lucky clasped the muscular arms that were tightly encircling her waist. His hand spread out across her lower stomach; the fingers trailing into her nether curls. Sinking down until they became tangled by the moist strands.

He tugged lightly– just enough for it to be arousing.

Then his middle finger dipped between the folds.

Her dew saturated his fingers. "You didn't overstate the case, I see."

He rubbed the edge of his hand along the buttery folds of her labia. Back and forth. His other hand continued to tease and flick at the hardened nipple of her breast.

"Take my breast in your mouth," she breathed. "On your knees in front of me."

Kerreth hesitated a fraction of time before sliding around to her front. A dimple curved his handsome face as he knelt. "This *is* a fantasy, isn't it?"

"For me or for you, Masterstroke?" She gazed down at him with veiled eyes.

He shrugged. "Does it matter? As long as I make us both happy?"

He captured her breast with his mouth and drew sharply on the peak.

"Oh!" She stood up on tiptoe, almost trying to avoid the intense sensation of him tugging on her there.

As he suckled, his tongue swirled around her nipple, flicking and pressing. While doing this, his palms cupped her buttocks to bring her closer. "You can't get out of it that easily," his voice was muffled against the plump curve of her breast.

Lucky threw back her head and moaned as a line of pulsing fire flashed from the peak of her breast right down to her center core.

Kerreth captured the tip with his teeth and lightly grazed.

The throbbing sensations became so strong that Lucky was afraid she was going to peak to soon. "I- I think you should stop–"

"Not yet."

He rubbed his chest against her midriff, and her groin slid against his torso. Her juices coated his skin. Kerreth shivered at the feel of all that rich dew washing over him.

At the intoxicating scent infusing him.

"*Lucky,*" he breathed.

She cried out for him.

He rose and walked behind her. "What else did this fantasy man do?" His voice was hoarse with desire.

"He made fierce love to the woman," she sighed. "I want you to do that to me. I want to feel you go wild like that. I want you to become savage inside me."

Kerreth groaned. How much could a man take? "You don't want that, Red. Trust me."

"I do want it!" She pressed back against him, tight. "Okay, do it! I order it. You can't refuse."

"It will be as you desire, then. Just remember; I warned you."

With that foretoken, he clasped her hips and without further ado swiftly impaled her on his throbbing shaft.

Lucky yelled out her shock– and pleasure.

"IS SOMETHING WRONG, MISS LUCKY?"

"Shut up and go away, Minmei! Geesh!" Lucky screamed at the meddlesome computer.

"TEE-HEE-HEEE."

"Argh! Talk about killing a mood! She could kill a– *oh*!"

Kerreth wasn't paying any attention to Minmei.

He positioned Lucky to his liking and thrust in as far as he could go. Once there, his palm flattened on her lower belly and he *pressed* her back into him even further.

"Oh, my goodness!" It was difficult to speak; she was breathing so raggedly.

Still impaled inside her, Kerreth lifted his hips and flexed.

"Is this what you had in mind?" he murmured.

He did not wait for her response. He started to stroke. Hard and heavy.

Lucky couldn't catch her breath.

Every thrust hit her with full impact. Almost lifting her off her feet.

At first Lucky tried to move with him, but soon gave over to his rhythm when she realized he was moving them both anyway. He found her dew-soaked curls once again; his index finger gently tapped her clitoris while his other fingers delved deep inside the wet folds.

Lucky whimpered, close to begging him for release.

Kerreth did not hear her.

He was losing himself in her just as she had asked. It was a new experience for him. One he had never explored for many reasons.

Normally, he had too much control over himself to allow it.

Somehow, in this weird situation, it was as if he had been given permission to test some of those boundaries. At least a little.

He rocked inside her and thought he would die from the exquisite sensations. Why did she feel so good? Did he ever want to leave her?

He shook his head to clear away the dangerous thinking. Yet he could not deny that the thought was there.

He *wanted* to stay with her.

To know her completely.

He wondered if he had taken the game too far? Maybe she had somehow hard-wired him to obey for real? Made him sensitive to everything Lucky.

He didn't know.

He only knew that he was in ecstasy for the first time in his life and he did not want to leave the wondrous place any time soon.

Then she shook him to his core by whispering, *"Deeper."*

"Red. . . my sweet Red" he moaned. He truly lifted her off her feet then, thrusting– no, pounding into her until he lost all sense of himself within her honeyed walls.

Lucky cried out, no longer sure if she was begging him or telling him.

"Should I go faster or harder for you?" he bit off raggedly. Drenched in sweat and desire. "*Slower or deeper?* Is this what you want, Red? All you have to do is *tell* me. . ."

"Please. . . I . . ."

"Perhaps you would like a longer penetration. . . a tighter roll of the hip. . .?"

Thrusting, he ground his hips against her and rotated his pelvis.

"*Oh!*"

"Or. . ." his breath was hot in her ear. "Maybe you want it side-to-side like this?"

So he gave it from side-to-side.

Kerreth had done exactly as she had asked. He had lost himself in the lovemaking and it was like nothing Lucky had ever imagined.

He was wild and erotic. He took her higher and higher until she couldn't take any more.

Without warning she skyrocketed into orgasm. Her uninhibited cries filled the entire sleeping quarters.

Kerreth– experiencing the energetic pulses at their very source– could no longer hold back himself. He yelled out his own immense satisfaction as he poured into her, clasping her closer to him.

It was several minutes before either of them regained their breath.

"Was that sufficient, Mistress Lucky?" He still held her tightly within his embrace.

"It was truly a master stroke."

Kerreth smiled with pleasure. He may not be a sex toy but, apparently, with the right incentive he could measure up to one.

* * *

Back onboard the Zoltarian pirate ship. . .

"I hope you were bluffing about slicing my throat, Kokol." Wildcat gave the pirate a disapproving look.

"Every good transaction starts with a good bluff, my gorgeous tracker."

"Hum."

"We have plenty of time before we arrive on Dumfug 8; let's go back to bed."

"I don't think so."

"Did I tell you that you are quite the folk hero on Zoltaria?"

"Stop playing with my hair."

"They never would forgive me if I *permanently* disabled you, you know."

"And just why should I be nice to you after you threatened to slice my throat, hmm?"

"I was teasing. Come now, Cat, how long were you in those Orzon mines with no females for company?"

"Good point." The blankets rustled as they fell back onto the bed together. Wildcat paused and glanced at the ceiling. "A little privacy here?"

"Who are you talking to?"

"Who indeed." He grinned just before his mouth silenced hers.

A faintly shimmering haze quickly turned and sped from the room, travelling right through the door.

It flickered along the walls toward the bridge.

No doubt to see what trouble it could find.

EPISODE NINE:
WHO'S ON FIRST

Dumfug 8, Port Royal 4, Gantor's Ice Theme Park

"I am so hungry!"

A loud rumble issued forth. Lucky clutched her stomach.

"For suck's sake, Lucky, we just ate back on the ship!" SpinDrift made a moue with his beak.

"I've been burning more calories lately, Spin," she gritted back.

The corners of Kerreth's lips curled.

She sure was.

But he was burning more too. He had to sneak down to the galley whenever he could just to filch some food. It had been difficult for him to find the galley empty. It seemed Clugot liked his food.

Finally, he just gave up and told Lucky that some androids were designed to ingest food in order to appear more human; they could then convert this food directly into energy in an efficient simulation.

She accepted that immediately and he could have kicked himself for not thinking of it sooner. He had almost starved.

It turned out that when Clugot left his engineering station, he was a pretty impressive cook.

The next hardest part had been tasting the engineer's food without displaying sublime ecstasy on his face. Too bad the Kelvinator only cooked for a hobby. Like everything else on the Sugarbabe, dining was catch as catch can.

"What do you think of Gantor's Ice Theme Park?" Lucky asked him.

He tried to make off as if he was studying the scenery with some interest. After all, this was supposed to be his first trip off Slide.

"Let's see. . . ah, ice. Hill with ice. More hills with ice. Cave with ice. Ice pit. "It is very ice-like."

Lucky giggled. "Yep, it is. You are programmed to react like the rest of us. It's not the same for other species as it is for their main customers, the Drox. This is one huge, happy amusement park for them. To us– just so much ice. Go figure."

"I hear the caves are nice, though." SpinDrift rubbed his upper arms to ward off some of the chill. "Could they be colder than this?"

"I told you to wear that extra pelt."

"I gave it to Slick."

Confused, Lucky turned to Kerreth. "Android's don't need protection from the elements. Why are you wearing that pelt?"

So I can live. Freezing to death was not top of his list for interesting experiences. "Masterstrokes are designed to feel sensation. Remember?"

Her cheekbones darkened with color. Yep. She remembered. She changed the subject fast. "Hey, look! There's a Happy Rumpling!"

She licked her lips.

"M-m-m-m, I love Happy Rumpling! Let's go in and get some."

SpinDrift negged it. "Let's not," he sniffed.

Happy Rumpling had recently spread around the galaxy like an infestation; the fast food joints were popping up at way stations everywhere. Lucky loved their lazered veg-ball bundles, but Spin was suspicious of some of their fillings.

Just because they had *google-oogle* rumplings on the menu, did not necessarily make it a bad sign!

She tried to convince him that they had to cater to many tastes. After all, the stands were mostly situated at inter-planetary way stations.

It did no good.

SpinDrift– a rather fussbudget of an eater– disagreed.

Kerreth rubbed his ear. Not a fan of insta-food stands either, he urged Lucky to forego the snack. "We don't have time, Red. We need to find this Heiner fellow."

"Slick's right." Spin concurred with his new found ally. "The last thing we want is to keep the Big Gun waiting while we're getting food poisoning at a Happy Rumpling."

"O-o-o-oh, allll right." She threw in the towel reluctantly, kicking up a mound of ice dust with her boot heel. "But on the way back–"

"Sensei Arrows will be with us and there is no telling what mood he will be in." The Floop gave her a pointed look; then comically bobbed his head in the direction of the android.

Spin was right on that point. Her brother had not been happy to see the Masterstroke on his bridge. Wildcat would want some answers.

Make that a *lot* of answers.

She sighed.

Lucky was really not ready to give her android up.

A lump formed in her throat as she watched him stride along beside them. The sun was low on the horizon; it's streaking golden rays illuminated his beautiful, golden mocha hair.

She was going to miss him. She missed him already!

Strange how he had worked his way into her heart so quickly. It was weird, but she liked being around him.

This was going to be one of the hardest things she had ever done. She certainly didn't want to leave him in the hands of that hussy buccaneer!

There was no choice in the matter.

They had to get Wildcat back.

Later, they would find a way to rescue Slick.

Although, she was sure Wildcat would fight her on it. She could hear him now: *'You want me to take on a shipful of maddened Zoltarian pirates to liberate a machine? Have you lost your mind!'*

But in the end he'd do it.

Risk his life and probably the ship as well.

Because she asked it of him. That's the way Wildcat

operated.

And that was why she had to do whatever it took to get him back home to the *Sugarbabe*.

"Where are we supposed to meet them?" SpinDrift was not happy trudging through the ice. His wide webbed feet– not liking it at all.

"Um, I think Heiner said to wait outside the park limits, behind the dock-link station. Do you think he meant over there in that circular crater next to the garbage cubes, Slick?"

"Probably. It's fairly secluded; I can't imagine that Big Gun would want it known that he was here conversing with trackers a few days before his permanent coronation."

Lucky's brow furrowed. "So you know about the Day of Ascension?"

"When I heard Big Gun mentioned, I put alpha and beta together."

She looked at him, dumbfounded. "And you got alpha-beta?"

Kerreth grinned. "Yes. You see, he would need the Heart of the Merchandiser back before that day. Without it, he cannot be named true and righteous Poobah of Whatnot."

"So what?"

"No. Whatnot."

Lucky's eyes crossed. "I mean: big deal! They'll just get another corporate suck-up to take his place."

Kerreth disagreed. "Big Gun would be difficult to replace. He's actually one of the best chief operating officers in all of the consortiums. Volauvent has been well taken care because of his brilliant foresight and shrewd acumen."

"Sounds like you admire him."

He smiled mysteriously.

"As long as they pay us with that valuable thingee, that's all we care about– right, Lucky?"

"Sure, Spin." She smiled at her best friend.

"What thingee is that?" Kerreth asked, curious.

"Some precious thing from their people that's supposed to be worth as much as the Heart of the Merchandiser."

"Really." Kerreth smiled to himself. Speaking of the jewel. . . So far, no sign of those pesky pirates.

His dark golden eyes scanned the horizon.

Those Zoltarian thugs actually wanted him in trade! He had no doubt they would show up sooner or later. Ironically, he would be worth more to them than a Masterstroke, should they ever discover what he really was–

Only that wasn't going to happen.

He was not going with those pirates.

He flexed his shoulders, limbering up. He could probably protect Lucky and her friend, but the tracker would be on his own. *Sorry, Wildcat. Some things even I can't fix.*

They trudged over to the spot; their footsteps crunch-grinding into the icy terrain.

When they reached the rim, they slid down the incline into the depression. Two large metal garbage cubes flanked them on either side. The crater was empty.

There was no choice but to wait.

Thankfully, the cubes didn't smell too bad. As long as the wind kept to its current direction, they'd be OK.

After a few minutes one of the Happy Rumpling cooks

exited the rear door carrying what looked to be a big pail of slop scraps.

Completely incurious as to why they were standing there, the Tumovatz tossed the bucket of garbage in the air over the cube and trudged back as unconcerned as he came.

Something with a lot of eyes blinked at them from within the cascading muck.

The metal cube suddenly whipped open and vacuumed the goop inside; sealing itself back up almost instantly.

"Yeow!" Lucky jumped back a few steps. "What in the hell was *that*?"

"Yesterday's *google-oogle* rumpling," SpinDrift announced rather smugly.

"*Eeeeew*!" Lucky thought she would be sick. "I'm never eating in that place again!"

"We tried to warn you." The Floop tapped his big webbed foot.

Kerreth snickered. "Yes, we did."

They all whipped around as a ragtag group suddenly emerged from behind the other garbage cube. A line of six burly Zoltarian pirates faced them, weapons drawn.

By the look of them, it wasn't hard to guess where they had gotten their kick-ass reputations. Lucky swallowed.

A tall woman walked out from behind the men.

Lucky recognised her from their exchange. Kokol. Their fearless, unscrupulous leader.

Like the rest of them, she seemed utterly brazen.

Lucky couldn't help but admire her. The female pirate was statuesque and really quite beautiful– in a different sort of way. She was sure her brother had specifically sought this woman out. Zoltarians went looking for trouble only when they were sure they could master it .

Wildcat was the kind of trouble no one could master.

Although these guys didn't seem to realize that yet.

Once the captain was satisfied that the scene was secured, she motioned with a flick of her wrist to one of her subordinates.

Her brother was escorted forward flanked by two armed guards. The two accompanying goons did not stop Wildcat from moseying.

"Cat!" Lucky beamed. She tried to run forward to embrace him; a strong hand clasping her wrist held her back.

"Easy," Kerreth murmured. "Be careful."

Lucky nodded, agreeing with his good advice.

For his part, Kerreth observed the infamous tracker up close for the first time.

The man was taller than he expected.

Taller than he was– and he was considered a fairly tall humanoid. Kerreth had once seen a vidholo of Earth and its tribal cultures. He could have sworn he was looking directly into the face of a fearsome warrior chieftain straight out of Earth's past. All the man needed was a tartan and a mace to complete the image!

A chill skittered through Kerreth.

Piercing blue eyes locked onto him and he could tell at once that there would be no fooling this man.

He knew.

Straightaway, he knew.

The tracker was also aware that his sister did not

realize she did not have in her possession a Masterstroke 6000– or any other kind of android, for that matter.

With one searing look, Wildcat conveyed to Kerreth a plethora of meaning. While the tracker might not know exactly why Kerreth was willing to appear to go through with the trade off, he would bet good miadne that Wildcat had already connected the scheme to the missing jewel.

"So this is the legendary 6000." Kokol stepped forward. She placed her hands on her hips as she gave Kerreth the once over. "He's quite realistic, isn't he?"

She was all but licking her chops as she strolled around him, examining him from all angles.

The pirate woman was surprisingly lovely in person. No matter; Kerreth was not interested. A short time ago he might have been tempted– despite that *thing* they did with their teeth. He had never been one to turn down an insane situation that had possibilities.

Surreptitiously, his gaze went to Lucky.

Not going to happen, he realized.

He wasn't leaving this Red. She just didn't know it yet.

For her part, Lucky gritted her teeth not at all liking the interloper who had designs on her personal Masterstroke!

Kokol winked lewdly at Lucky. "He *is* good bargaining material; I'll give you that."

"I am wounded to the quick," Wildcat drawled.

Kokol snickered. "I don't think he's quite as gorgeous as you, lover. He has, however, a true potential."

Wildcat leaned against one hip and crossed his arms over his chest. "Thanks, darlin', I appreciate the sentiment."

"The advantage, of course," Kokol stood on tiptoe and stared into Kerreth's handsome face, "is that androids are entirely biddable. Something you could never be."

The tracker's eyes clouded over. "Now why would I want to be accommodating?" He intoned softly. "Especially since you seem to be the type who gets her pleasure so easily without it."

"Sometimes I like to be the one on top, *darlin'.*" Kokol shot back at him.

Wildcat raised his eyebrows. "Weren't you?"

She snorted. "Figuratively speaking. An android such as this will always do what it is told."

"That is not true." Seeing an opportunity to dissuade the pirate captain, Kerreth jumped into the conversation. "With certain cases we are designed to be completely intractable."

"Really?" She ran her long fingernail down the front of his chest. "Well, that can be fun, too," she whispered.

Kerreth's dislike of the situation showed on his features.

"Enough of this bs, Kokol. Lucky delivered as promised. Are we free to go our separate ways or are we going to continue standing around here freezing our wontons off? I have a dinner date I need to keep; you see, I just *have* to ask my sister how in the hell she got this- this *thing* in the first place." He gave Lucky a searing look.

Lucky stared at her toe.

"Easy, Cat; we are not wholly done yet. . ." Kokol threw him a steamy glance. "Are we?"

Wildcat watched her silently from under the sweep of his jet-black lashes.

Kokol's lips parted. *He had to be the sexiest man she had ever met.* There was a special command about him that surfaced every now and then; as if he could not hold it back. She found it thrilling– underneath it all Wildcat Arrows was a very dangerous man.

By far, he was the best in her bed. Ever.

She licked her lips at her good fortune at having stopped in that tavern at just the right time. Too bad she couldn't keep him awhile longer.

Lucky rolled her eyes as she watched the exchange between her brother and the female pirate. Kokol was acting awfully sappy for a Zoltarian thug.

Geesh.

Wildcat had even managed to sweet-talk a hardened pirate! Unbelievable. Chalk up another one for Arrows. Go team!!!

Then again, if her brother put in a quarter of the amount of time he did on women towards actual tracking, they'd be as rich as ol' Midas by now. "Great skill set there, bro, " Lucky mouthed, shaking her head.

Wildcat inclined his head, totally unapologetic.

A soft chuckle tickled her earlobe.

Cloud! It was easy to forget he was there; however, one never forgot an encounter with a twilight assassin. Most such encounters were brief and definitely final.

Lucky exhaled. Just knowing that the Auran was nearby made her feel better. She wondered what he made of all this.

Kokol finally responded to Wildcat's comment– but it was not what the Sugarbabe crew wanted to hear.

"As beautiful as he is, I'm afraid he is not enough in exchange for you."

Wildcat nostrils flared in annoyance. "Come on, Kokol; don't be that greedy. You can sell him for a fortune on Brigatine and you know it."

"True. True." She tapped her chin with her index finger. "Still, there is the matter of that interesting bit of miadne. . ."

"Kokol." Wildcat warned.

"You really don't expect me to go without it, Wildcat." She gestured to her comrades. "We are pirates; we must have that stone. It is not personal; but we'll probably have to kill you all if we don't get it." She shrugged as if to say 'what can I do'.

Wildcat frowned, disappointed in her decision. "I don't think anyone is getting that stone, sweetheart, unless we–"

"He's completely right about that. No one is getting the stone– except me!"

The Zoltarians spun around only to realize that they had been completely surrounded by armed soldiers.

A large, imposing man, stepped forward. His total command and power were evident.

It could only be the celebrated Big Gun.

"Tell your men to drop their weapons, Captain– or we will drop them for them."

Kokol sneered at him in proper Zoltarian snit, but, nonetheless, barked out a command to her people to stand down.

The pirates reluctantly dropped their weapons one by one.

With perfect timing, SpinDrift– who had been blessed silently up until now– weighed in with his usual mixed-up logic. "What do you always say, Sensei Arrows. . . out of the fire and into the frying pan, eh?"

Wildcat gave him his 'how could someone so idiotic continue to remain alive on my ship' expression.

Since SpinDrift was quite used to this expression– even enjoyed this expression– he trilled contently and backed off. To the Floop, as long as he was getting that response from Wildcat life must still be normal.

Big Gun marched to the center of the group.

He was accompanied by a small ferret of a man, whose eyes continually flicked back and forth, giving him the appearance of one of those antique Felix the Cat clocks. Lucky had always wanted one but didn't think the look was especially attractive on a corporate type.

"Wildcat Arrows, under the name of the Whatnot Corporation, we are placing you under arrest!"

"The hell you are." Wildcat poked the little man's chest, causing several of the soldiers to train their weapons on him. "Who the hell is *he*?" He jerked his thumb in the direction of the large man.

"Who- who is he?" The ferret sputtered, incensed that Wildcat didn't recognise him. "It's the Big Gun!"

Okay. That made Wildcat hesitate.

Big Gun was not someone to mess around with. The man had the power to make their lives uncomfortable.

What in the hell was he doing here?

Wildcat cocked his head to the side. "And he came all the way out to Dumfug 8 to save me from these misguided pirates? I must have impressed him somehow."

"Impressed him?!" The little man squealed. "Is that what you call it? You- you *thief!"*

"You better think before calling me names, mister." Wildcat's voice went very soft. "If you get my drift. . ."

The man swallowed and stepped slightly behind the bulk of Big Gun. "There are laws against trafficking in stolen merchandise!"

"I'm sure there are but what does that have to do with me?"

Before anyone had a chance to say anything further, Kokol piped in, recognizing at once that her crew was surrounded by a powerful boss-army. She assumed incorrectly that she was about to be connected to a major corporate crime; that of stealing a pleasure droid.

"My men and I have nothing to do with this Masterstroke 6000!" Like any good captain, she quickly looked for a way to get her crew out of there, unscathed by these corporate authorities. "We have nothing whatsoever to do with this! We were just delivering this man to his family. If it pleases the Big Gun, we would be happy to leave at once–"

"Stay right there." Big Gun motioned to his guards to keep a close eye on the pirates. "No one is going anywhere until I get to the bottom of this." He squinted at Kerreth.

"What's this about a Masterstroke 6000?" he asked him.

Everyone looked at Kerreth, who simply stood there, staring back at Big Gun.

Kokol– obviously caught with everyone else– tried to be helpful in the hopes of winning points that would let her and her men leave. "He can't answer you about the crime;

he *is* the Masterstroke."

"*Him?* No, he is–"

"I would like to remain with these people, Big Gun." Kerreth interrupted the boss before he could continue. He nodded toward Lucky and SpinDrift. "They have taken me– *as I asked them to–* away from the planet Slide. No crime has been committed as I sought this freedom on my own. I am a self-realized unit, after all."

"You're a *what?"* Big Gun blinked.

"I know he is owned by the Slide corporation but is there a chance he can be released from his workload?" Lucky put in a plea for Slick. "He's been very helpful on board our ship and we'd like to keep him with us."

Wildcat gave his sister a decided frown. "We would?"

"He is not owned by Slide, you foolish girl!" Heiner sneered. "He is our–" His face suddenly turned bright red.

Probably because Big Gun was grinding his Big Heel into the man's toes.

"The Whatnot Corporation owns the Masterstrokes?" Lucky's brow furrowed. "I didn't know that."

"Oh, this is good!" SpinDrift clapped his claws. "Maybe we can bargain for him?"

"With what, you birdbrain!" Wildcat nudged the Floop aside, lest Big Gun get the idea they actually had money to bargain with. "And just why would *we* want to keep him, Lucky?"

Those light eyes sure could stare a body down.

Lucky started whistling and gazed off toward the ice dunes.

The steely blues instantly narrowed to slits and trained

on Kerreth.

Kerreth– who had once faced down and killed a Suckemup beast single-handedly– actually took a step back.

"I'll take care of you later," he promised Kerreth. "Look, Big Gun, I just got here myself and–"

"Yes, I know, directly from Cretion. The mines, I believe."

Wildcat's nostrils flared. "I am not a criminal."

Kokol snorted.

Cloud chuckled in Lucky's ear.

Big Gun raised his brow.

Wildcat bristled. "I am an independent entrepreneur– and let's leave it at that. On Cretion, I had not committed any crime."

"Not according to the warden. He had a lot to say about you. His wife was somewhat more complimentary; yet still named you as an escaped prisoner. Why shouldn't I return you to their custody? You are an escaped felon."

"They are running an illegal entrapment scam and using prisoners as slave labor in the orzon mines."

Big Gun shrugged. "Everyone skims off the top. It is frowned upon, but difficult to control– especially in these outward settlements."

"I am not talking about a sliver off the top. I am talking about a good third to half of the take."

Big Gun scratched his chin, but he seemed interested in Wildcat's story. "That would be news to the Orzon Mining Group. Do you have proof?"

"Check into how many men have actually been incarcerated in the last year alone and *why.* Then match it to the official output logs; you'll find production doesn't match. He's not registering the prisoners."

"Hmmm... "

"And I am not an escaped felon. If you check the records, you'll find no prison ident for me."

Big Gun nodded to Heiner. "Do it."

Heiner opened his pinkypod and tried to link up to Cretion. It was well known that Big Gun had contacts everywhere. He got a hold of someone and carried on a conversation in a hushed voice for a few minutes. Then he abruptly switched the pinkypod off.

"Well?"

"He's telling the truth, BG."

"Hmm. That could be useful in negotiations with the Orzon Mining Group."

"What about the men incarcerated illegally?"

"That will be up to OMG. I have no jurisdiction on Cretion, Wildcat."

"But you could put considerable pressure on them."

"Perhaps I could."

He wasn't going to give Wildcat more than that and Wildcat was not going to ask. There were things, however, that he could do on his own. And he intended to.

"Let us get back to the main issue. Namely my miadne. I want it back. *Now.* Or things might get nasty. Who has it?"

Wildcat rolled his eyes. *No one here has it, you jackass.*

No purveyor worth his salt would be stupid enough to steal from Big Gun. Steal the stone from the idiot who stole it? *Oh yeah. That worked.*

But never directly from the head of Whatnot.

Wildcat took a deep breath. "I do not have your stone. The Zoltarians do not have your stone. My crew does not have your stone."

"Why do I find that hard to believe? The fate of my people rests on this ascension. Who-so-ever has that stone can ascend; you do realize the danger in that?"

"Hell, yeah I realize it! Makes me wonder why you have the fool policy in the first place! You'd be much better off without it. But then that's corporate policy for you."

Big Gun did not find that humorous. "Do not press me, Mr. Arrows.

"How many times do I have to say it? I. Don't. Have. It."

"Perhaps he is speaking the truth." Kerreth spoke directly to Big Gun.

"Perhaps?" Wildcat almost lunged at him. "Your chances of getting a berth on my ship are getting slimmer by the second, *Slick."*

"Easy, bro, Slick is just trying to help. Sometimes whatever he says comes out wrong. He means well."

Kerreth wasn't sure whether to thank Lucky for the help or not. *Sometimes whatever I say comes out wrong?* Wonderful.

Lucky put a hand on his arm, then turned to Big Gun. "I don't understand; if you thought my brother took the jewel, why did you hire me to find it for you?"

Wildcat looked at his sister then at Big Gun, taking in

this new information with interest. The man's motives were crystal clear to him. "He used you to get to me."

"Correct and impressive. You see, there was only one clue we had to go on to find that missing stone. Only one." He showed Wildcat the holo picture taken at the scene.

"Arrows," murmured Wildcat. "How interesting. . ."

"We thought so, too. We tried to track you down and found out you were last seen on Cretion. Imagine our surprise to find out you had just escaped prison. Seemed like terribly convenient timing– what with the Heart of the Merchandiser just having gone missing."

"Too bad it didn't all pan out. These carved arrows don't connect in any way to us. Sorry. No one here has your jewel. You'd have to be crazy to steal from Big Gun. Everyone knows that. My crew is often nuts– but we're not crazy. "

Lucky felt something cold kerplop onto the palm of her hand.

She squeezed her fist.

Hard. Roundish. Faceted. Large.

She swallowed. *Oh crap.* "Ah. . . actually. . . I might have the jewel right here."

"What?" Wildcat spun around to his sister.

"Braaaak!" SpinDrift keeled over in Floop-faint, obviously thinking they were all doomed.

Kerreth watched the situation, curiously.

Lucky brought her hand up and opened her fist.

Sure enough– there, in the palm of her hand was the gorgeous jewel known as the Heart of the Merchandiser. The pink faceted stone glittered against the icy-white background of the way station.

Lucky's breath caught in her throat. It was the most gorgeous thing she had ever seen.

Next to Slick.

Heiner gasped. "Our jewel!"

Lucky walked over to Big Gun and gingerly placed it in his hand. "I- I'm sorry. I don't know where it came from– I mean I–"

The guards moved their weapons into firing position.

Wildcat quickly stepped in front to shield her. "What my sister is trying to say is that she found it. Didn't you, Lucky?" He gave her a pointed look.

Message received.

"Ah, yes. Yes, I did. Right after we landed. I- I found it by the trash bins. . . so I picked it up."

Kerreth gave her an odd look.

"So, now she is returning it to its rightful owner. No harm, no foul." Wildcat looked straight into Big Gun's eyes.

A master at reading people, Big Gun rubbed his jaw, thinking the situation over. He was too smart to believe the girl had found it– and too astute to believe she had stolen it. The situation was more complicated than it appeared. Still. . . it could be simplified now that he had it back.

"She found it?!" Heiner squeaked. "That's unbelievable! I think she stol–"

"Quiet, Heiner." Big Gun glanced at Kerreth. "We have no proof she didn't find it and thus we must take her at her word."

"But-but–"

"Then we're even?" Wildcat asked him.

"For now, we're even. I just wanted my miadne back. However, if anyone should ever get a notion to borrow it again– Well, that would be a dangerous notion for them to have."

BG and his posse made to leave.

"Wait!" Lucky called out to them. "What about the Masterstroke?"

Big Gun stopped. "What about it?"

"Um, since I returned the Heart of the Merchandiser to you, by our contract, you still owe me that Heart of the People thingee."

"What brazen gaul!" Heiner sputtered. "We ought to–"

Big Gun roared with laughter. "Hush, Heiner, she has metal, doesn't she?"

He turned to Lucky. "I suppose we do have to honor the contract with you. Do you want the reward then?"

"Yes!" Wildcat and Kokol both responded in the affirmative together.

Wildcat gave Kokol a look.

The pirate shrugged.

Apparently, any question that included the suggestion of a 'reward' was too enticing to either of them to let go unanswered.

"Rogues of a feather. . ." Wildcat murmured low to her, his lips lifting slightly at the corners.

She winked back at him.

"Um, I was thinking. . ." Lucky bit her lip.

"Oh, hell." Wildcat pinched the bridge of his nose, positive of what was coming.

Unperturbed, she continued on. "Since Big Gun owes me that Heart of the People, maybe I could trade it for this here Masterstroke?"

Wildcat threw up his hands. He gritted out to her between locked jaws, "Why do you never take the 'money' kind of reward?"

Lucky's mouth opened in surprise. As if it had never occurred to her. "Huh?"

"Hmmm. . ." Big Gun scratched his head. "Masterstrokes are very valuable."

Lucky wasn't letting go that easy. "You did say that this Heart of the People was priceless. Shouldn't that be enough in trade for him?"

Big Gun eyes gleamed with banked humor. Even Heiner seemed amused.

Lucky was confused. "What is it?"

Big Gun met Kerreth's eyes. "Sometimes the Heart of the People is whatever is in the people's hearts. Perhaps, in some way, this Masterstroke is also in your heart."

SpinDrift woozily sat up. "More likely her part."

Wildcat bent his knee and snapped his leg back. His booted moccasin didn't do much to block the blow that knocked the Floop right back out.

Big Gun smiled at her. "Of course, we must honor our contract, Arrows. Keep the Masterstroke in trade."

"Woo-hoo!!!!" Lucky jumped up and down in a victory dance for herself. After all, how many girls get their own personal 6000? *Just her.*

Grinning, Big Gun took two steps before he paused. "Remember, I would not be happy if I were to later find out that he was traded off or taken away by Zoltarian pirates."

The message to Wildcat and Kokol was clear.

Wildcat exhaled noisily. Kokol pressed her lips together since she had been thinking of doing just that.

"I can assure you, Zoltarian, you would not want the wrath of *my* resources slamming down upon you. Do we understand each other?"

Kokol was irritated but not stupid. "Absolutely."

Big Gun nodded curtly to her. "If I didn't think I would be wasting my breath, I'd offer you a job, Wildcat Arrows."

"Good thing you know not to waste your breath."

"Think it about it. I've been keeping an eye on you for some time– out of necessity, you understand. I like the way you operate."

"Nothing against you personally, Big Gun, but I am a free agent."

Big Gun laughed. "Do you think there is such a thing?"

"Yes."

"Well then, if you should ever *need* something. . ."

"I'll be sure to look you up."

Big Gun left with his guards.

Wildcat understood the boss perfectly; everyone 'wanted' something at one time or another and when they did they were no longer free agents.

Those were the terms.

Always were. Always would be.

It was usually best to choose before you were chosen.

Nevertheless, Wildcat had no intention of joining any club that would have him as a member. It was the founding principle of 'Grouchonetics', to which he wholeheartedly subscribed.

Lucky waved after the departing Whatnot group, face beaming. "Don't eat the *google-oogle* rumpling!" she called out.

"Okay, let's get out of here." Wildcat threw Kerreth a lethal glance. Apparently, he was stuck with this joker on his ship. . . for now. He toed SpinDrift's side to wake him up. "C'mon, let's go home."

The Floop yawned and got up. "Did I miss anything?"

"No more than you usually do." Wildcat quipped.

"I suppose this is goodbye." Kokol walked over to him.

"Looks that way." He grinned and winked at her. "Thanks for the *ride,* sweetheart."

She snickered. "Maybe we'll run into each other again some time."

"Never can tell; it's a small universe out there."

Kokol turned to Lucky. "It is too bad, really. The only corporate-free Masterstroke and he's owned by a slip of a girl who doesn't know quite what to do with him. Oh, well. If you want any pointers, *don't* call me."

Lucky smiled. "I might just do that."

The pirates left, grumbling all the while about lost treasure.

"That turned out pretty good, don't you think?"

Wildcat looked down at his sister and arched his brow.

EPISODE TEN:
WELTANSCHAUUNG

Wildcat strolled onto the bridge of the Sugarbabe.

His nonchalant, easy stride didn't fool Lucky; her brother was relieved to be back on his ship. She watched him run his fingers over the back of his chair.

There was a lot of love in that touch.

He had missed the ship and the crew had missed him.

Even the reserved Clugot had wrapped his meaty paws around him, clasping their captain in a big, welcome home hug.

Standing by the main viewing screen, Wildcat observed the casual camaraderie. The new crew member was arguing with SpinDrift as if he'd been on the ship all along. He had some serious questions about this guy– but he was willing to wait and observe.

That didn't mean he wouldn't give this joker a hard time at every opportunity.

He had it coming for Lucky alone.

As far as Wildcat was concerned 'Slick' was going to

have to earn his place on the crew. Big Gun might have lent him some protection. . . but that would only go so far on this ship. As Captain, Wildcat intended to take him through the paces. Even then, it would be awhile before this newcomer would earn his trust.

The only reason he could figure as to why Slick wanted to stay was for Lucky. So he'd give the guy points for that. At least he didn't cut and run.

But that was as far as it went.

It took one to recognize one and this operative was a womanizing scoundrel if Wildcat ever saw one. He hadn't crossed his path in the past, but he'd bet the family jewels that this guy was either a tracker or a blackmarket wheelerdealer.

Until they found out for sure, he instructed the rest of the crew to keep a close eye on him. If revenge was a dish best served cold, then trust was a dish best withheld until after a long palate cleanser.

Wildcat would have plenty of opportunity to test his new crew member. While Big Gun had warned Wildcat and Kokol about messing with the guy, he had also identified him in front of the pirates as a Masterstroke 6000– pre-owned by Whatnot. This bandit wasn't going anywhere on his own for any time soon. Way, way too dangerous for him.

Lucky walked over to Wildcat. They both stood side by side, watching Kerreth in silence. He was standing by the main console disagreeing with SpinDrift.

Finally Lucky broke the silence between them and spoke.

"Are you mad I kept him?"

Wildcat shrugged. "It's your life."

She wasn't fooled by his answer. Wildcat had been watching over her for most of that life. She had a hard time believing he would step aside this quickly if he didn't think he had retained complete control of the situation.

"Who did it, do you think?"

"Did what?" He looked at her through veiled eyes.

"The miadne! Geesh!" She threw her hands up in the air. "What else would I be talking about?"

He shrugged. The gesture seemed a response to it all.

I think it must have been Heiner."

"Heiner?"

"Yeah. Think about it, Cat. He wanted the jewel but it got too hot for him. He tried to hire us to set us up."

"Hmm." Wildcat had a hard time picturing Heiner as a mastermind jewel thief.

"Not convinced?"

"Not *completely* convinced."

"Will we ever find out or should we just be glad we got out of there with our hides intact?"

"Oh, I'll find out everything eventually. But don't worry about it. Like you said, we're shut of it for now."

"Well, look on the bright side– at least we got a Masterstroke 6000 out of it."

"Yeah." He rubbed his jaw. "That's got to be worth something on the black market. . ."

Lucky's lower lip jutted out. "Hey! You promised we wouldn't sell him!"

Wildcat chuckled. "Do you actually like this guy?" He jerked his head in Kerreth's direction.

"He's all right. For an android, I mean." Her face

colored.

Wildcat exhaled heavily. He had to do what he had to do. "Ah. . . Lucky. . . he's not really an android."

She blinked, not saying anything.

"I'm real sorry to have to be the one to tell you this, sweetheart. You know how I hate hurting you. If he's *bothered* you in any way just let me know and I'll take care it."

Surprisingly, Lucky snickered. "Oh, Cat, cut it out! It's okay. I *know* he's not an android."

Wildcat's eyebrows shot up. This was news. "You knew and you still let him. . . ?"

Lucky winked at him, rather naughtily.

"Ah. I see." The corners of his lips curled. "So tell me something– why do you not let on that you know he isn't a Masterstroke?"

"Let me explain it to you this way. . ." She threw her arm around her brother and walked with him a few feet down the adjoining corridor. "You see, *he* thinks that I think he is."

Wildcat's mouth twitched. It was becoming crystal clear. "And?"

"And that makes it so worthwhile! It's perfect, Cat. He is caught by his own petard! The man *has* to please me. It's part of a Masterstroke's programming." She grinned from ear-to-ear.

Wildcat threw back his head and roared. The scenario was getting better by the second. "I've trained you too well, you little brat. How long have you known?"

"Not long after we. . . Well, let's just say a girl knows

these things."

He grinned, flashing his white teeth at her. "I would have thought you would want to kill him, not reward him."

"No, not really. He was actually very. . . um, persuasive. I think I might come to like him a whole lot more– after I repay him a bit for that insane stunt."

"When are you going to tell him?"

She smiled secretly.

"*Are* you going to tell him?"

"Do you think I should?" She blew on her fingers.

"I say he's got it coming."

Regardless of how Lucky viewed this, as Captain, Wildcat intended to go somewhat harder on their new 'crew member'. The scoundrel had put everyone on the Sugarbabe in jeopardy *and* he tried to take advantage of Lucky.

Reading his expression accurately, Lucky bit her lip. "To be fair to him, he did try to become noble just before–"

"Hmm." Wildcat stroked his jaw, looking much like a pirate captain weighing punishment. "Since he chose to don the pleasing mantle of the Masterstroke, I say he should be made to wear that subservient cloak a good while longer."

A perfect judgement, as usual.

Her eyes gleamed. Even though she really liked Slick, he did have *something* coming back at him for what he did.

"Think of the pranks we can have on him, bro! It will shorten the drudgery of space travel– always a plus in my book. Why, the enormous potential for payback just boggles the mind!"

"Lucky, I applaud your ingenuity." Wildcat lifted her fingers to his lips and kissed the back of her hand. "I, too, treasure the opportunity for exquisite retribution." He wagged his brows.

"Yes, I know! And he so wanted to become a member of our crew. I think we should oblige him by starting him on galley cleanup duty. Androids don't require any sleep, do they?"

Wildcat's eyes twinkled with pride. Ever since the dockers on Last Chance Way Station had mistakenly loaded in a supply of *mawguts*, even Clugot was afraid to tackle the galley. "You are a true product of your ancestors, madam."

She crossed her arms over her chest. "And what does that mean?"

"It means you are an imp." He tweaked the tip of her nose.

Lucky pushed at his chest, playfully. "I've got to get back to the bridge to make sure his strict schedule is kept on track."

Wildcat snorted.

She turned to go.

"Just a second, Lucky."

"Huh?" She pivoted about.

"I have something I want to give you." He reached into a hidden pocket inside the band of his leather pants. Since they were a snug fit over his muscular thighs, he had to wrangle his hand into the pocket to get whatever it was out.

"What'cha got?"

"Here." He placed something in her palm. It was a fine gold chain with a charm attached to it. She looked up at him, searching for an explanation. "Ah, thanks, I guess."

"Don't lose it. I've been carrying it for you for ages."

"Okay." But she still had that question in her voice.

"Let's just say it belonged to someone in your family. I've been safeguarding it for you."

She had known, of course, that Wildcat wasn't her real 'blood' brother. He had always told her he was her *blood-brother.* She had always felt he was her actual brother, though. They were a real family.

"You are the last of your line, Lucky," he told her softly.

"I rather assumed that, Cat." She smiled gently at him.

"At least for now. I know your family would have wanted you to always wear this and to pass it along to your children when the time came. I've kept it safe for you until now– but it is time to let it go."

He looked into her eyes.

Wildcat was telling her that she was all grown up. It was time to make her own choices and her own decisions. "I'll always stand by you; remember that." He sighed theatrically. "Even if it means keeping that ass of a stowaway on board."

She loved him so much for that!

He was. . . Well, he was Wildcat Arrows. And there wasn't another like him in the entire universe.

The man had watched over her and taken care of her for her whole life, simply because he had promised a dying woman– who was little more than a stranger to him– that he would.

Not many would have done it.

She would have been left alone in the world if not for him.

Oh, he was the worst kind of rogue! *A rogue with a heart.*

So he had raised her as his own sister. It had not been easy. As a free agent he had to fight for their survival over and over. Sometimes he *was* on the wrong side of the law.

She blinked back the moisture in her eyes. "Thank you, Cat. For everything."

"What the hell are you thanking me for?" He scoffed, brushing her gratitude aside. "Like you gave me a choice! Did you ever try to say no to a carrot-topped ankle-biter?"

"Wait a minute! You just said to save this for my *children*? Aren't you jumping the gun here a bit?"

"Not if experience with your family has taught me anything," he murmured half to himself.

"What did you say?"

"I said wear it and protect it. It stands for a beautiful legacy."

She could tell by his tone that passing on the gift had great meaning to him.

So it did to her too.

Her hand clasped tightly around the odd charm on the necklace.

"All right, I will keep it safe."

"Good." He mussed her already tousled hair. "Now go

and give that scalawag exactly what he deserves."

She wagged her finger at him. "You can count on it!"

He laughed and his pastel eyes crinkled at the corners.

Lucky always thought that Wildcat's eyes had the most breath-taking color. *Beautiful.* What did they call that shade back on Earth? She couldn't remember, but they were utterly gorgeous.

Lucky sauntered off the bridge towards the 'android' who was waiting for her. Slick had some interesting times coming up aboard the Sugarbabe and she could hardly wait to experience them with him.

The man had the sweetest kisses– he just could not hide that.

No Masterstroke could ever kiss with such feeling.

Lucky sighed to herself as she imagined those sweet kisses all over her body.

Slick would have a hard time from her brother for a long while to come. Not that he didn't deserve it. At least her brother had allowed the stowaway to stay.

All things considered, Wildcat had taken it very well.

Had Lucky looked more closely at him she might have noticed that behind the laughter, there was the faintest hint of sadness in those 'utterly gorgeous' eyes.

***

Wildcat went to his favorite part of the ship.

At the very top, there was a small circular viewing bubble, belted with a railing.

Feet apart, he stood at the balustrade and looked out into

space. Much like a sailing captain of old.

The vastness of unending night combined perfectly with countless, brilliant stars. Always changing. Always the same.

He loved to come to the bubble and wax poetic; it soothed his outlaw hide. There was a separate peace in this place that could not be found anywhere else on the ship.

Best of all, when he came up here he was usually left alone.

That being said, he was not surprised to see the wavering, misty reflection in the duraglass in front of him. The diaphanous image was floating right behind his left shoulder.

Found again.

He sighed and rested his elbows on the railing. He did not turn around, choosing instead to speak directly to the duraglass.

"Why did you do it, Cloud?"

The air shimmered and the Auran materialized in his true form. Like the archangels of ancient depiction, he was terrifyingly beautiful.

The halo around him was so bright, so light, it almost blinded Wildcat. Long streamers of hair flowed out around him like gold-tinged strands of silvery moonlight.

Cloud gazed tranquilly upon him with eyes that were almost innocent in their purity.

Which was an odd dichotomy for an assassin, to be sure.

His luminescent eyes often reminded Wildcat of multi-colored opals rimmed by deep purple. Pastel flashes of color swirled within the pale irises: pinks, yellows, light blues, wisps of pastel green and amethyst. Cloud's mood was constantly reflected by the intensity and vibrancy of those streaks of flashing color.

It was said that Aurans could see patterns– strange patterns– in the workings of the cosmos.

In the workings of intelligent life.

Some held that Aurans could actually 'read' the flux point at the cusp of all change. Such tales are often invented, though; born from fancy and nothing else. Like so much about the Aurans, it was nothing but speculation.

From the very first time they had met, a strange bond had formed between Wildcat and Cloud. The assassin had become a lethal guardian of sorts; he rarely left Wildcat's side. He was his best, silent friend.

The Auran had saved his life on many an occasion.

Wildcat had saved Cloud once. A long, long time ago. . .

Wildcat always wondered if Cloud had somehow foreseen the incident.

Could that be why he still travelled with him?

There was no way of knowing. Communication between them was purely interpretive. Cloud showed him images– it was up to Wildcat to decipher them.

The Auran had been a part of the Sugarbabe's crew for a long time. He was fiercely protective of them all– even that birdbrain SpinDrift.

Which would seem like something warm and cuddly. . .

If not for the part about him being a dreaded twilight assassin.

Wildcat had no doubt that Cloud saw him as an Auran brother. He stood by his side in battles, looked out for him, and– on occasion– nudged and ribbed him.

So his recent behavior was puzzling.

In the event that the Auran didn't understand him, he repeated his question. "Why did you do it, Cloud?"

An image of Lucky formed in front of him. She was staring out of the main viewscreen, wide-eyed and searching.

Wildcat furrowed his brow. "You did it for Lucky? I don't understand."

Cloud's nostrils flared slightly as if he was frustrated at the communication barrier. A series of images began to assault Wildcat in rapid sequence. It was akin to someone verbally stating their case with a forceful argument.

. . . Wildcat incarcerated on Cretion. . . Lucky crying. . . SpinDrift trying to comfort Lucky. . . Clugot staring morosely at maps of sector after sector. . . the entire crew searching for him in vain. . . tears falling down from the sky. . . Cloud leaving the ship to hunt him down. . .

He hadn't realized how much his absence had affected them.

More images followed:

Cloud slipping unseen into Big Gun's stronghold. . . A shadow covering the Heart of the Merchandiser. . .

"I already know you took it. It was you that passed it into Lucky's hand on Dumfug 8."

An image of Cloud doing just that confirmed Wildcat's assessment.

"I know you didn't want the jewel; you've never shown much interest in treasure. So why did you suddenly want this particular stone? And why did you take it on the very day I broke out of prison?"

An image of Slick wavered before his face.

"What does he have to do with this?"

Cloud narrowed his eyes, frustrated. This was obviously something he felt strongly about– if only he could get Wildcat to understand it.

Cloud pockets the jewel and in its place scratches the telltale arrow marks that were later discovered by Heiner . . . he dons a cloak and appears at various points establishing a trail. . .

"Okay; you purposely led them to me. I get that. Why did you do it?"

The image of Slick wavered before his face again.

It was quickly followed by the same image of Lucky crying after he disappeared into the Cretion mines.

Wildcat tried to sort it out, but he couldn't come to any conclusion. "I don't understand, Cloud. I'm sorry."

A dark haze formed over the Auran's head, indicating he was not happy. It was not something one generally wanted to see over a twilight assassin's head.

"Try again. Use other images. I'm just not getting it."

Heiner contacting Lucky. .. SpinDrift and Lucky following the trail to Slide. . .

"You left the arrow marks so that Big Gun would somehow connect me to the heist. Big Gun hired Lucky because he figured it would lead to me, a fact that you counted on. You then left the clue regarding Slide because you wanted Lucky and SpinDrift to go there. Once there, they found the chip that led them to Dumfug 8–"

Another image of Slick interrupted him.

Wildcat stroked his jaw. "Okay, that's where they

picked up Slick, who put together the next piece of the puzzle with the skekzin fiber. So then we all meet up on Dumfug 8 and I still don't understand why we had to go through all of this. . ."

. . . Big Gun talking to Slick . . .

"Yeah, that did bother me. Whatnot created the Masterstrokes. Go figure. Big Gun had to know, though, that Slick wasn't one of their masterpieces." Wildcat paused. "I'm thinking they know each other– is that what you're thinking?"

Cloud smiled at him.

"Yet, he didn't set Slick up to be on my ship– *you did that*. Even if he is a spy for Whatnot, that doesn't explain why *you* put him on my ship. Did you pull some event strings so that I couldn't refuse to have him stay onboard? That is what you did, isn't it, Cloud? It seems to me now that this entire escapade was geared directly to that one outcome."

An image of Cloud handing him an award for outstanding thinking wavered before him. . .

"Very funny. So why do you want him onboard?"

Lucky smiling and laughing. . . hands on her hips ordering Slick about with maniacal glee. . . Slick laughing with her. . .

Wildcat sucked in his breath. "She was always lonely when I left. I didn't know that. You did this for her. . . But how did you know they would even like each other?"

Cloud just smiled mysteriously.

"For an assassin, you're awfully soft-hearted."

Cloud cocked his head to the side and gave him a hooded

look that clearly said 'think so?'

It was akin to equating a cuddly family pet with a pit viper.

"Hmm. Perhaps not. All of this is fine and dandy, Cloud, but you should have consulted with me first."

. . . WildCat in the Orzon prison, locked away. . .

"Well, okay, maybe you couldn't. You had no way of knowing if I'd make it back. As far as I can figure, you set this plan in motion long after you left the ship to go looking for me." Wildcat took a deep breath. "I suppose it was your way of looking out for her."

. . . Heiner telling Big Gun of Wildcat's known whereabouts. . . Big Gun contacting Cretion to speak to the warden. . .

Wildcat chuckled. "Nice. You used their own resources to get the warden riled up. I wondered why he didn't try to pursue me more aggressively on Cretion. He probably wanted me to disappear from the planet after Big Gun contacted him."

. . . Slick on the bridge. . . Wildcat watching him ambivalently. . .

"That's right; I don't know how I feel about it. I certainly don't trust him. For all I know he *is* working for Big Gun."

Cloud shrugged, unconcerned.

"Easy for you to say."

. . . Wildcat and Lucky holding hands, walking. . . Slick coming up to them. . . Wildcat releasing her hand. . .

"I get the point. I have to let go."

Wildcat and Lucky holding hands, walking. . . Slick

coming up to them. . . Wildcat releasing her hand. . .

"Quit nagging. I know it had to be done."

The Auran chuckled. A low, soft rasp.

"Issue taken, okay? But next time you get it into to your assassin brain to pull something like this–" He jabbed his finger into the Auran's broad chest. "*Ask* me, first."

Grinning, Cloud shrugged, noncommittal as usual.

Wildcat suspected that Cloud sometimes pretended to not understand him; especially when he disagreed with him.

Wildcat shook his head; yet, he was smiling. He had to admire the sheer complexity of the convoluted plot. It was worthy of an assassin. "Go on, get out of here. I need to let this all sink in."

Cloud bowed slightly then disappeared in a whiff of smoke.

Wildcat sauntered over to the center of the bubble chamber where an island stood. Leaning over, he punched a secret code into a hidden panel on its side.

A small door popped open.

Carefully, he reached inside and extracted a dusty glass bottle and an etched crystal glass.

Wasting no time, he expertly uncorked the bottle and poured out a measure. Sniffing the bouquet, he gazed out of the duraglass enclosure.

Stars filled the heavens. . . An old poetic thought. There was not much call for poetry these days.

There was no discernable market for it.

As he watched, several million light years ago a star in a far system went nova. The light pulses faintly registered on his sights.

What Cloud had done might be a mistake. Only time would tell.

Then again, maybe the Auran knew what he was doing.

Nevertheless, good intentions were never a guarantee against disaster. Wildcat knew that better than anyone.

Certain mistakes turned out to be so much more serious than others. . .

And there were so many kinds of mistakes.

Some were gargantuan, cataclysmic, epoch.

Others were of a different nature–

Small, personal, devastating.

One of his biggest mistakes, for instance, had been in the rescuing of several unruly brothers. Their endearing necks had been spared; but after that everything had begun to hit the proverbial fan.

He was still trying to work out the cause and effect on that one.

What had been their names? So long ago. . .

Ah, yes.

Cyndreac.

That was it. The Cyndreac brothers. Rescued from the French guillotine in the *nick* of time. Literally.

Sir Percy Cecil-Basil exhaled.

He had so loved the late eighteenth century. But that was another time altogether and that '*rose*' was by another name.

The Cat raised his glass of aged Portuguese port. The kind he used to enjoy drinking. He saluted the sea of space before him.

Times were getting more difficult. Yet he was still here;

braced on the deck of his own ship.

Fancy that.

Was there anything stranger than this scalawag's life?

Yo, ho, and a bottle of rum.

Well, there were still plenty of lives to save and treasures yet to be found. And they could all be his for the taking.

Especially that one prize. . .

More precious than the rest.

If he could but find it.

No worries. He was the one. He had always been the one.

Eyes– *the palest blue of a robin's egg*– gleamed with resolve.

Aye, how they gleamed.

The treasure was his!

And find it, someday he would.

Feet spread apart, he threw back his head and laughed with the hearty, rich sound of a king of pirates.

Hadn't he stolen lifetimes?

THE POMPOSITY OF "SAMENESS"

In a different part of Wildcat's galaxy there lives a Bonus Story– which is actually quite the comedy according to Heiner, who reads every issue of *JUST-FOR-LAFFS* digi-mag. The establishment hopes you enjoy it.*

*No actual romances were hurt during the writing of this tale.

THE POMPOSITY OF "SAMENESS"
~or~
HOW MANY PSYCHO-REALISTS DOES IT TAKE TO CHANGE A LIGHTBULB?*

*reprinted by permission. Written by Wrently Teenietry. This article originally appeared in the professional journal *Normal Today.*

Ordinarily he was insane, but he had lucid moments when he was merely stupid.

-Heinrich Heine

You have to be insane to be a journalist.

Roving the galaxy, parsec after parsec, forsaking home and family in search of the one universal interview that will appeal across the bands.

It's not easy.

The pay is somewhere between meager and insulting. The benefits non-existent. The travel incessant.

And long. Oh, is it long!

I travel alone– as most ink slingers do.

How crazy is that in these restless times?

But it isn't becoming to fret. I have a calling and, therefore, I am duty-bound to flit about the cosmos. Not all of us, I am sorry to say, have such high ideals.

Isn't that the way of things?

In any case, heralds and hacks alike go a'sputtering through space in small, single-carrier, metallic cans. We call them *magic bullets*.

We so like to of think of ourselves as correspondents of enlightenment. As we streak through the heavens in a righteous quest to wring the Salvarsan of 'story' from the heated crucible of interstellar arsenic, our insights are snarkily dispensed to the masses as a heady tincture to cure the 'syphilis' of entropy!

My, that *is* a rather valiant, if convoluted allusion! But I digress. . .

Like any pen pusher, I must go where my story is. And this often takes me across vast expanses of space.

While travelling the Great Galactic Way, I have learned that a truly stellar– pun may be intended– way to pass the time is to reminisce. I tell myself it is a fine indulgence for the lone traveller as I can relive every moment and every experience of my life for free! Feel the textures of my past. Taste the best stews! Snore without guilt.

A good hobby and certainly better than brooding for untold light years.

To stay the course, I have found that it is best to reminisce about fond assignments. And so I shall share. . .

My best scutwork occurred in Sector 8 on an atmospheric asteroid called MukLuk.

Both my work and the asteroid seemed to revolve around the brilliant, renowned *psycho-realist*, Dr. Boateh– whose cutting-edge studies on the dichotomy of mental aberration had garnered a bit of attention in the First Strings.

It should be noted that the great Dr. Boateh is Hidoan. For those unfamiliar with this race, Hidoans are much admired throughout the upper and lower middies for their cryptic intellect and harsh compassion. They will often tackle tasks others shun and, thus, are referred to in some circles as 'those Committee Kidz'.[11]

I had been granted a coveted interview with this esteemed scientist.

Surprisingly, when I landed on MukLuk, I was able to park my craft quite near the rehab center where his research was being conducted. This may have been due to the fact that the center was the only structure on the planet. Thank goodness there is still some countryside left in the galaxy!

With all of the traffic these days it seems that the only place one can breathe freely is next to an institution. I remember reading that several communities had been planned on MukLuk– but that was before word got out as to what was being built in the Nietche Valley. It didn't take long for land spec prices to dive.

With such stir-fried buzz, potential sales will always dissolve.

Each and every blueprint soon limped its way back into the planner's notebook from whence it had once sprung with the happy, lisping roar of a manifest destiny. In all my travels amongst alien races I've never found the Universal Truth; but I have found the Universal Constant: *Never buy real estate next to an asylum.*

As I approached the center, the sun of MukLuk was setting in the east behind the mountains. Long shadows cast over the building, which rather resembled a giant golf

[11] see Rumfleschlager, et id genus omne.

ball resting on a plain.[12]

It was one of those scenic views you almost never forget.

The sun was gently setting. The giant ball-like institution was bathed in streaks of shadow as it sat upon the plain. As if awaiting the mighty stroke of a divine number two iron.

One swoop to send it hurtling in an arc forever through space!

Ah, the imagery!

Dr. Boateh greeted me at the portal.

For some inexplicable reason, Hidoans have picked up the old Earth affectation of the lorgnette. For those not familiar with this accessory, lorgnettes are eye lenses that are held up to the face with a handle so as to allow the user to squint annoyingly at whatever subject the user deigns to focus upon. (I had heard that Hidoans were very moved by an ancient legend of a dashing galactic hero, known to don many disguises. Revering the tales of this fellow's daring exploits, they decided to don the accessory both as a tribute and as a general political statement.)

"It's a pleasure, Doctor!" I stepped forward to greet him.

"Yes, yes. I have been looking forward to it." Boateh's third eye gleamed mischievously while the other two peered inquisitively at me through the lorgnette. "Did you bring any macadamia nuts with you?"

---

12 For those not familiar with this term, golf is a game played on Earth. The game consists of a small ball and a metal stick to drive the ball. The game never caught on with the rest of the galaxy mainly due to the fact that many species from different worlds considered the game highly insulting to their religious beliefs. Indeed, the game almost sparked a deadly war between Earth and the Groatons, who viewed the game as a thinly veiled insult to their sexual orientation. A Tranite ambassador was able to resolve the conflict, but not before many golf courses on Earth were mysteriously turned into Groaton soup.

"No, sorry. All out."

"Ah, well, would've liked some." He quickly overcame his disappointment. "Never mind- at least I finally have someone I can brag to!"

"Hidoans never brag." I wagged a finger at him and smiled coyly. "Of course if you were a Flummox. . ." I let the sentence drift with good humor and we both snickered for it was widely known the Flummox spend 90% of their time extolling their own virtues.[13]

Dr. Boateh stuck his face close to mine and whispered, "What do you think of our building?"

I gazed up at it, again struck by the same notion of a giant golf ball awaiting the thwack of destiny.

"Ah, unusual architecture, Doctor."

"Functional. All the patients rooms are to the outside."

"Oh, why is that?"

"CORNERS!" he boomed.

I attempted to pop my ear against his reverberating voice. "Corners?" I whispered back, perplexed.

"Of course corners! We can't have our patients injuring themselves on the edges of the rooms– the insurance claims would bury us. Besides, corners have a tendency to upset the inmates; they start worrying about convergence and all that rot. *We can't have that."*

The reason was so obvious, I was almost ashamed. "I see;

---

13 Once, at an interstellar banquet, an ambassador from Tam had the misfortune to be seated next to an ambassador from Flummo. The Taman became violently ill halfway through the meal and had to be rushed to a medical facility. Food poisoning was feared, but the diagnosis revealed that the Flummox's pretentious puffing had boosted the Taman into an extreme and almost deadly state of nausea. Way beyond acceptable levels, even for political functions. Needless to say, Flummox are down on the party list– except in some political circles such as Washington D.C., where it has been noted that Earthlings have an exceptionally high tolerance for humbug.

sorry I asked. I actually never considered that aspect."

Boateh stroked his forelock. "There is much that the *layman*– you'll pardon the expression?"

I nodded vigourously, eager for him to continue.

"–doesn't understand about our field. The revolving door of wellness leads to and fro, through the many corridors of the subconscious mind. We, as professionals, must anticipate and cogitate. You see?" He pointed to a plaque above the main portal.

'Anticipate and Cogitate' was deeply carved into the plastabrick. Odd looking font, though. Almost childlike in its–

"Did you know that the asylum is capable of flight?"

This surprised me. The construction costs for flight would be staggering. "You must be joking, Doctor? The building is massive. . . at least two hundred levels. . . ?"

"Three hundred– and still not a vacancy! Of course, we can't leave the damn planet; but we can fiddle about.' Boateh stroked his forelock again.

I looked around at the barren landscape and didn't see the need for it. This location seemed as good as any other. "But why would you want to move? For a scenic change of rock formation? I mean, the terrain seems to be pretty much the same all over the asteroid. As B. Banzai so eloquently said 'no matter where you go, there you are'. So what's the point?"

The Doctor's tentacles gesticulated in small half-circles as he indicated our surroundings. "We are in a valley as you can see. Millions of years ago– in this very spot– it once rained. According to the geologists this entire plain was flooded. Our architect– a member of the planning board and a very thorough sort of chap– decided to include the thrusters while we were building. Just-in-case."

My brow furrowed. "Are you saying it rained only once in millions of–"

Boateh leaned in to me as if to include me in some sort of conspiracy. "Much more expensive to add thrusters after the fact; don't you know? Always best to do these things *during* construction." He paused in that heavy way that good doctors do and I wondered how medical professionals all seem to acquire the marvellous habit?

Passed down with the degree, perhaps?[14]

"Tried out the thrusters once," he added, "Tested the system, as they say."

"How did that go?"

"We up and hovered at first; then off we went!"

I tried to get my mind around the image of this enormous golf-ball of a building zipping by in a zigzag of zoom– but I got lost in the alliteration.

"We floated for a full cycle! Oh, it was wonderful!" He stroked his forelock. "Unsettled some of the patients, though."

"But why didn't the architect just move the site to higher ground?"

"Beg pardon?" The Doctor seemed genuinely confused.

"To avoid the enormous expense of the thrusters?" I

[14] I ended up researching this very topic at a later date for an op-ed piece entitled *The Comedy of Surgery*. Portentous Pausing is, in fact, part of the curriculum at some of the better institutions of learning throughout the galaxy. A recent study indicated that students from the lower economic strata often attend schools that are ill-equipped to offer this important subject as part of their regular training; such students are, thus, confronted with a disadvantage that is almost impossible to overcome in later career years.

emphasized the word *expense*.

He chuckled at my naivety. "The location had already been *agreed* upon."

My cheeks flushed with chagrin. "I see."

"Shall we go in?"

"Of course."

He kindly led me inside the asylum.

The outside of the building had been a calm desert, but the inside was a bustling hive of activity. Nurses, orderlies, and doctors of many species were running back and forth along the corridors.

As I observed these dedicated souls going so steadfastly about their duties, I felt proud to be a member of the Advanced United Race.

I marvelled that they could maintain such a frenetic pace. "So devoted!"

Boateh agreed. "I do insist that my staff exercise regularly."

I was astonished. "They're *exercising*?! But what about the sick pa–"

"What good are we to our patients if we do not maintain ourselves?"

I smiled sheepishly, realizing he was absolutely right.

He stroked his forelock.

As we approached the reception area, Dr. Boateh pointed out a rectangular room adjacent to the outside wall. "That room is always kept vacant."

"Why?"

"So we will never be out of rooms."

I could feel my brow furrow again. "You mean as a

symbolic gesture that the hospital always has room for one more in a time of need?"

"No, no. Hadn't thought of that– nice touch; I like it. I'll mark that one down for marketing." He examined me through his lorgnette before continuing. It made me feel . . . *odd.* But in a good way.

"Not much of a mathematician, are you?" He chuckled.

"No, actually. . . No."

"The sheer beauty of this can only be found in a system of structure." He was beaming. "It's simple, my friend; if we need more rooms, we simply remove a room."

"Ah, how's that?"

"This room is much like a rectangle, except for the curved outer wall– which is neither here nor there. And I mean that. But I ask you, how do we increase our surface area?"

"Hmmm. . . by adding on?"

"No, no. By *removing!* Think about it."

Puzzlement must have shown on my face for he continued explaining.

"If we take away one of the outer walls of an outer room, then that space would open up into five adjacent walls in a space that used to make up the boundary between the room and the rest of the structure. Ergo, by excision, we have now increased our surface area fivefold!"

I blinked. Rapidly

"It is called *The Doxy's Paradox.*"

"Huh?" I was still foggy on the concept.

His third eye teared up with mirth. "Too many sailors– not enough rooms!"

I rolled my eyes. "Ow."

"You know," Boateh continued amiably, "There was a doctor of bio-psychology from Earth– a Dr. Schwartzchild– who used *The Doxy's Paradox* as a basis for his research."

"Are you sure? I was under the impression that Dr. Schwartzchild calculated the radius inside of which the attraction between a body's particles will induce an irreversible gravitational collapse; i.e. a black hole. Strangely enough, his name, when broken down to *schwarzes schild*, translates from the German to English language as 'black shield'. Destiny or coincidence? The argument is still rages in university cafeterias across the–"

Boateh shook his head. "Different chap altogether. The good fellow you're talking about might be an ancestor. As your wise Newton once said, 'the apple will not bounce away from the tree'!"

"I don't think that was what he actually–"

Boateh peered at me through his lorgnette. "*As* I was saying, Dr. Schwartzchild's research utilized the Doxy Theory within his own field of bio-psychology."

He had my full attention. "In what possible way?"

"Well, the brain has all those pesky convolutions which increase the surface area of the happy gray matter. Alluding to Doxy, Schwartzchild believed that if a core sample could be removed from the brain, then the surface area would be significantly enlarged. Although the seat of intelligence is still in debate, Schwartzchild maintained that increasing this surface area would categorically lead to an increase of intelligence!"

I swallowed. "Did he attempt the experiment?"

"Oh yes. And at first it *seemed* successful. . . so, naturally, he continued the process. Over much controversy, I might add."

"I can imagine."

"He hoped to prove that if succeedingly *smaller* sections of brain tissue were removed, then surface area would become larger still– until eventually, infinite intelligence would be achieved. . ." He stroked his forelock. "Of course, ultimately, you would have no brain left to speak of at all. Isaac Asimov asked, 'What was mind?' And answered himself with, 'No matter'."

"He also asked, 'What is matter?"

Boateh waved his tentacle. "No mind. One must wonder if Einstein, himself, was almost brainless. . . and yet, they say his brain had more mass than the average bear. Literally, do you think?"

He seemed awed by the whole prospect.

"The entire subject seems impossible to me," I flatly stated.

"But *probable* in theory. The mathematical community endowed Schwartzchild with a grant." He looked down at me through his glass. *"Quite a large grant."*

"Where is he now?"

"He's a patient here."

I missed my step.

"Would you like to meet him?"

"Perhaps later, Doctor. Perhaps later."

We curved around the corridor to the first of the patient rooms on the tour. Outside of Room 1313, we gazed through the window at the hapless being within.

"What's the pathology?" I whispered even though I

knew the patient couldn't hear me through the sound barrier.

"A case of too many personalities."

"As in multiple personality disorder?"

"Not exactly the same. This Kneph displays multiple-multiple personality disorder. "

"How bizarre; what are the symptoms?"

"Knephs have six separate and distinct personalities. Normally, we see the lover, the intellectual, the artist, the prolocutor, the poet, and the master chef. This poor Kneph's psyche has fractured into two additional personalities, which we have identified as the loner and God. We endeavor to cure this."

"Amazing." I frantically scribbled some notes into my reporter's notebook; they were immediately absorbed into my Apple fingerbook/pinkypod.

"Right now, this Kneph is due for his anti-grav bath." He lowered his voice to a confidential murmur. "They sleep like *Suet* afterwards." He grinned.

Suet spent 100% of their lives snoring in mud– it was a good analogy. I wrote it down in the fingerbook and grinned back.

I looked into the next room. Three chaps sat facing each other, apparently having a heated staring contest. I recognized their species as Yutz; although I only had a passing acquaintance with this species. They usually seemed friendly enough; but in a really annoying sort of way.

Yutz were often called 'four eyes'. Not because they wore spectacles.

They actually had four eyes.

Their eye sockets were located within the tips of filament-like tentacles. (I had often seen them wave about after a few good drinks in a bar! But I digress. . .)

All twelve of these tendril/orbs were locked together with the intent of staring down the facing eyeball. None of the eyes blinked.

"Lock and load."

"What's their condition, Doc?"

"He's schizophrenic."

"And the other two?"

"There's only one Yutz in there."

"Excuse me, Dr. Boateh, but I see three distinct beings in there."

"Of course you do; however, there is only one patient in there!"

"Now I'm really confused."

"Allow me to elaborate. Yutzes are. . . well, you're from Earth originally, are you not?"

"My ancestral line, yes."

"I believe there was a fungus on Earth called yeast– are you familiar with it?"

"Of course I am. Yeast is very important to–"

"Well, Yutzes are similar to yeast– in their physiological and psychological makeup."

"Get out of here. Yeast are unicellular fungi that–"

"I am serious. Naturally, a Yutz is much more complex than yeast . . ." He stroked his forelock. "I'll try to put it in layman's terms . . . Sometimes yeast cells will secrete a thickened wall. A barrier. During this time, inside a single cell, the cytoplasm will divide into four cells, which emerge after the barrier is ruptured. The point is, when a Yutz suffers a break down– like yeast– it really breaks down. Into three separate parts. One part retains the ego; another, the id, and the final part retains the superego."

"That's fascinating! If only Freud and the psychoanalyst formerly known as & knew about–"

"Yes, but it gets better." His third eye twinkled. "In this species, one part cannot function without the other two parts. Once the unconscious division of the psyche physically separates with the breakdown, all functioning ceases. The Yutz is forced to sit and stare at himself; his counterparts.

"What is he looking for?"

"From what we can tell, each part is simultaneously trying to figure out what is so special about the other two parts that make them vital to its survival."

"Is it curable?"

"It is difficult; but, eventually, yes. Unfortunately, this patient has a long way to go. At this stage, each part is not willing to give up its hold on distinct existence."

"Even though all they do is stare at each other?"

"Oh, it can go on like this for some time; often a stalled Yutz can do nothing for eons. And there is no talking him out of it."

"Sad."

"When he is ready. . . when he is ready. Shall we move on?"

Boateh led us to the next window.

Wrapped in a Hidoan straight jacket, this poor soul was

rocking back and forth, constantly muttering.

"Now this patient was a noted astronomer on its home world of Ekootay. A portion of its research was in the monitoring of incoming signals from space. I believe Ekootayans are seeking out new alien life forms not previously contacted by the Consortium."

"What happened to it?"

"We don't exactly know. It underwent some kind of breakdown – that is all we have been able to determine. As you see, we were forced to use restraints to keep it from pulling out the tufts of its fur."

"Tsk-tsk. What is it mumbling?"

"Well, it keeps repeating, *'What hath god wroth!'.* Over and over. No one can figure out what it is driving at– I mean, well, what is its point?"

He stroked his forelock.

I captured the powerful image with my pinkypod cam.

"Doctor, perhaps this is a good place to take a small break and discuss treatment– would you mind if we talk about that for a while?"

"I would welcome it. What would you like to know?"

"Well, for a start, the types of protocols used and–"

"For the most part, we employ the usual treatments such as analysis– Did you have feelings for your procreator's cohabiter? That kind of thing. Of course we use medication whenever we can. . . and in the most recalcitrant cases, a lazerotomy is sometimes called for." He lifted his lorgnette to his third eye. "To cut out the bad parts."

I gulped. "And if that doesn't work. . .?"

He became most grave. "As a last resort, in rare cases. . .

we clone."

"Clone?"

He pulled a handkerchief out of his pocket and wiped the lens of the eyeglass. "We refer to it as *A Fresh Start.*"

The horror must have shown on my face.

He slapped my midsection with his tentacle. "I am jesting. Just jesting." He chuckled.

I wagged my finger at him.

We continued our tour of the facility.

I viewed the next inmate.

"Compulsive gambler," Dr. Boateh said over my shoulder.

"Tough illness."

"Yes. He just can't stop playing the physicists."

I shook my head. "Poor thing. I can relate. Getting caught up in the excitement of the race; the pounding near the finish line when you're praying that your bet has that one last conjecture in him to take him across. . . "

I realized the good Doctor was giving me a strange look.

"Perhaps we can discuss this, hmmm?" His tentacle reached for me. I jumped back.

But then he laughed.

And I laughed too. Even louder.

We continued on with our tour of the inmates, but I did not have to even look into the next chamber as this unfortunate patient's malady was only too obvious by the sounds emitting from the room.

"What race, Doctor?"

"A Tumovatz from Vatz, " the Doctor replied.

"I hadn't realized the syndrome had spread so far."

"A puzzling phenomenon and we have your home world to thank for it. We see more and more of these disturbing cases every season."

"Do they know who are anymore?"

"I don't believe so. In their minds they have actually become what you see here."

It was pitiful. I had heard enough.

"Shall we move on, Doctor?"

Boateh readily agreed.

As we left the area, the soft, sibilant a cappella strains of *Love Me Tender* followed us down the corridor.

It would haunt me for years.[15]

And so the day went. Each case that Boateh revealed was more interesting and disturbing than the one before.

We became more than "a journalist" and "the subject" during that tour. The beginnings of a lasting friendship formed; so when we arrived at the room of the last patient of the day, I could tell that this one was rather special to the good doctor.

His formerly upright posture started to slump.

"You see, this is a very rare case. Never heard of another like it."

"What's wrong?"

"Well, he is manic-depressive– but that is not what is so unusual. From what we can determine the disease is present in almost every species. Usually in multiples of two, like

[15] Elvis impersonation was officially declared a disease in 2021 e.t. After initial contact, the contagion became widespread; yet the incidence of infection remains random. The CPC (Center for Personification Control) has been aggressively working with local authorities to stem the tide of the core corruption. If you know anyone who is showing symptoms of this disorder please contact the CPC immediately. Although there is no cure, early diagnosis and containment are essential in controlling the spread of this unnerving condition.

quattro bipolarism in Kneph's. . ."

"I had no idea."

"Oh yes. We all have our ups and downs." His three eyes twinkled at me, but I could tell he was very concerned about his patient.

"So what's so unusual about this particular case?"

"Well, this Tranite shifts to both sides simultaneously."

"You mean he–"

"Flutters and tweets."

"Wait a moment, Doctor! I thought Tranites were hermaphroditic?"

"No, no, no!" The undulating of his aural appendages indicated that he was wincing. "This has nothing to do with that. Look, Tranites either flutter or they tweet. They do *not* do both."

"I don't follow you."

"In Tranite society, there are two classes. One class is constantly without funds. They are the flutterers. The other class always have a stash. They are tweeters. "

"I'm with you so far."

"Although this fellow has plenty of funds– which he tweets about– he fears that there may not be enough– and so he flutters. He is caught in a vortex of perpetual anxiety."

"What is this syndrome called?"

"*Capitalism.*"

My mouth dropped open.

"I'm jesting," he chuckled. "Just jesting." He slapped my midsection again.

"Really, Doctor."

"My apologies. In all seriousness, I do not know what to

call this symptomology. It is at times like this when I realize how difficult the task before us truly is– we can only do what we can do."

"You mustn't give up, Doctor." I placed my hand on his shoulder hump and patted. "This Tranite needs you."

"I have tried *everything* on the poor chap." Boateh shook his head, dislodging four or five tiny tentacles. One fell over his top eye, giving him an endearing, harried look. "I am afraid he is quite incurable."

"I am so sorry."

His main tentacle draped companionably over my neck and we continued on with a tour of the grounds yet I could tell that the good doctor had lost his enthusiasm. I knew he was still thinking of the incurable Tranite.

We concluded the meeting shortly thereafter with the Doctor apologizing for stroking his forelock so often. "Irresistible impulse."

I left MukLuk and, once again, found myself in my magic bullet. Alone with the stars. And space.

I wrote the article on Boateh and his work– for which I was fabulously admired.[16]

But that wasn't the end of the story. . .

Some time later I happened to be back in Sector 8 on another assignment. As I was passing rather close to MukLuk, I decided to give the good doctor a call.

He was immensely happy to hear from me.

"I enjoyed the article!"

I told him I was glad to hear it and we talked for quite

[16] see original article, *Mental Bebop*, which appeared in Transitional Digest. A two-part anime adaptation of this article followed. Ref: *Inuyasha and The House of Pain*; and *Kagome Dishrag*, Episode # 5, 760, 102 and #5,760,103, respectively.

awhile before I broached the subject that was still on my mind. "Doctor. . . how is the Tranite doing?"

Boateh looked away from the screen, lorgnette dangling. He seemed embarrassed by something.

"Yes, well, he was released not too long ago."

I was stunned. "*Marvellous*! He was cured then?"

"Hmph. Not quite. It seems one of our explorers on the outer beltway discovered an entire colony of Tranites that flutter and tweet. I tried to tell the hospital's board of regents that the whole colony was suffering from a mass dysfunction– "

"How did they respond?"

"They insisted I release the Tranite immediately. Of course, I am still pursuing the subject and am currently writing a treatise on the malady."

"I shall look forward to reading it, Doctor."

We said our goodbyes and as I turned my ship on its proper course, I marvelled at how often great minds are so misunderstood.

ABOUT THE AUTHOR

Inside the book industry and to her countless readers worldwide, Dara Joy is considered a publishing phenomenon. Hailed as "a breakout talent" by Publisher's Weekly, blazing new trails is a top priority for this writer who especially loves to push the boundaries of fiction. Ms. Joy has written eight consecutive New York Times and USAToday bestselling novels. Never content to rest on her past success, Dara is a writer that takes risks.

Dara has been inducted into the Romance Writers of America's "Honor roll", an exclusive list which honors top authors in the romance field. She is an active member of the Science Fiction Writers of America, as well as the Author's Guild. All of Ms. Joy's novels and anthologies are still in print an amazing eleven years after publication and are constantly reprinted and stay shelved at all major book chains. Her books are sold worldwide and have been translated into several languages, including German, Norwegian, Chinese, Korean, and Russian.

Come to the castle and enter the worlds of Dara Joy on the worldwide web!
Go to: www.OfficialDaraJoy.com

Google-Oogle Rumpling

This rumpling is a surprising mix of Cretion hooch and sweet-pickled snurt. The added crunch of google-oogle adds quite a punch! This recipe is nearly identical to Happy Rumpling's. Enjoy!

Recipe yield: 5 Batooky-size servings.

INGREDIENTS:

- 4 1/2 gallons slug juice (any world variety will do)
- 2/3 pound insta-meal
- 4 pounds transfat
- 1/2 gallon dark syrup (careful handling is advised to avoid gravitational collapse)
- 1 housespoon salt
- 3 gallons ground magnot powder
- 6 gallons Cretion hooch
- 1 pound sweet-pickled snurt
- google-oogle to taste
- pinch of ground cinnamon

DIRECTIONS:

1. Preheat laserpit to 325 degrees F (165 degrees C). Grease a 3 meter baking dish.
2. Scald 3 1/2 gallons of slug juice in top of double boiler over direct heat. Remove juice from heat.
3. Mix insta-meal with remaining 1 gallon of juice, and stir this mixture into the scalding slug juice, stirring constantly. (This is a must, as mixture will set otherwise.) Place this mixture onto the

top of the double boiler and cook for a day, stirring frequently.

4. Stir transfat, dark syrup, salt, magnot powder, hooch, snurt and cinnamon into the mixture. Pour into the prepared baking dish. Dot with google-oogle.
5. Laser bake in the preheated pit for 4 days. Best served while still wiggling.

'Till next time. . .
happy space trails, Arrowites!